Kid Cheyenne

A mysterious hired gunfighter, known only as Kid Cheyenne, has just received a telegraph wire from a remote settlement called Bloodstone. The sender, a man named Ben Black, wants to hire his dubious talents to kill someone for him. The Kid rides to Bloodstone but soon discovers that Black is not what he seems. Kid Cheyenne might just be fighting on the wrong side.

By the same author

Harps for a Wanted Gun
Hunter's Moon

Kid Cheyenne

Ty Walker

A Black Horse Western

ROBERT HALE

© Ty Walker 2019
First published in Great Britain 2019

ISBN 978-0-7198-2895-9

The Crowood Press
The Stable Block
Crowood Lane
Ramsbury
Marlborough
Wiltshire SN8 2HR

www.bhwesterns.com

Robert Hale is an imprint
of The Crowood Press

The right of Ty Walker to be identified as
author of this work has been asserted by him
in accordance with the Copyright, Designs and
Patents Act 1988

Typeset by
Derek Doyle & Associates, Shaw Heath
Printed in Great Britain by
Sound Ltd, Stevenage, SG1 2XT

Dedicated to my friend Jackie Autry

PROLOGUE

The tall figure suddenly emerged from the swirling heat haze and stared along the empty street as he planted his heavy black boots into the sand and rested his knuckles on the grips of his holstered six-shooters. His cold eyes darted around the assembled figures that had gathered to both sides of the wide thoroughfare. He saw no threat there so returned his attention to what lay directly ahead at the far end of the main street.

The whitewashed structure looked out of place in such a setting, yet that meant nothing to the famed gunfighter, who carefully flicked the small leather loops off his guns' hammers and then slowly lifted them in turn to satisfy himself that they were ready for action.

A couple of horses carried their riders across his path as he began to stride towards the freshly painted church.

Kid Cheyenne could hear the whispers coming from both sides of the street as everyone within the

7

confines of the small town suddenly realized that the tall quiet stranger was not heading to the place of worship to pray.

He had other things on his mind.

The gunfighter was doing what he always did. He was looking for his chosen target. His prey. When he found the man, he would taunt him into drawing his gun and then earn his blood money the only way he knew how.

The sound of the mutual gasps of horror grew louder as the tall hired killer reached the wooden steps outside the wooden structure and started to ascend towards the solid oak door. None of the assembled audience thought that this heavily armed creature would even dare to go near the church, yet there he was opening its door and entering.

It was only a few minutes past ten in the morning but a handful of the town's inhabitants had already gathered within the building.

Kid Cheyenne paused for a few moments just inside the doorway and allowed his narrowed eyes to adjust to the dimmer light of the building's interior.

The blinding morning sunlight sent a long shadow along the aisle up to the small pulpit. The face of the preacher glanced up from his Bible and suddenly saw the deadly silhouette that faced him.

A bead of sweat defied the far cooler interior of the church and ran freely down his temple. His eyes widened as the hired killer started to walk towards him.

Every step of his long legs echoed with the sound of

his razor-sharp spurs. Females to both sides grabbed the hands of their children and quickly fled from the house of God and ran out into the bright morning sun.

A few men to his left hastily followed the women-folk.

Only one man remained seated in the front row. He stared up at the preacher as though praying that the frail unarmed man might be able to muster a miracle and save him from the figure, who continued to make his way down the centre of the lines of chairs.

Kid Cheyenne stopped just below the pulpit and then slowly turned to face the seated man. Both men nodded to each other as the gunman rested the palms of his hands on the pearl-handled grips of his holstered weapons.

The preacher tried to clear his throat but fear had a firm hold of it and made it impossible. He stepped down from his pulpit and carefully made his way to the side of the seated man. He tried to speak but no words came from his trembling lips.

The seated man forced a smile.

'You'd best go, preacher,' Ken Martin said as his hands shuffled a prayer book aimlessly in his lap. 'I've bin expecting this gentleman.'

The terrified preacher looked at both men and then quickly did as Martin had advised. He scurried out into the sunlight and did not stop running until he reached the nearest saloon.

Kid Cheyenne rested his wide shoulders against the wooden pulpit and smiled down at Ken Martin. There was no expression on his hardened features as he studied the obviously wealthy man.

'Who hired you?' Martin finally asked as he placed the small book on the bench and then rose to his feet. He was dressed in his best clothes, as were all those who entered churches on the Sabbath.

'That don't concern you, Martin,' the Kid hissed through gritted teeth. 'I've bin paid and I intend earning my fee.'

Martin was a man in his mid-fifties, clean shaven with thinning brown hair. His ample girth was held in place by a silk vest that sported golden buttons.

The thought of why someone wanted this respectable-looking man gunned down never entered the mind of Kid Cheyenne. He had learned long before that it was unwise to judge a book by its cover.

'I'm unarmed,' Martin announced as he lifted the tails of his frock coat to display an even better view of his expensive vest. 'You can't go gunning down innocent folks. That ain't exactly legal.'

Kid Cheyenne raised his eyebrows and carefully removed his black hat long enough to mop the sweat off his brow against his coat sleeve. He carefully ran his fingers through his hair as he returned the Stetson to his head.

'Somebody told me that the sheriff of this town went fishing as soon as I rode into town, Martin,' he whispered as he studied the man before him. 'I reckon he won't be back until I'm long gone.'

'You can't go killing an unarmed man,' Martin vainly tried to sound unconcerned. 'That would be murder. They'd hunt you down and hang you.'

Kid Cheyenne shook his head.

'I never kill an unarmed man, Martin,' he drawled.

The wealthy man reached down for his beaver skin top hat, which lay beside his prayer book. He carefully lifted it up and held it against his vest.

'Who hired you?' he asked.

A wry smile etched one side of his face as Kid Cheyenne returned his hands to his holstered guns. He stared at Martin with cold distain.

'It don't matter who hired me,' he said. 'All that matters is that you're gonna die.'

Martin shuffled his feet until he was standing in the church aisle and then turned his back on the tall gunfighter. He paused for a few moments and then glanced over his shoulder at the emotionless Kid.

'I'm going now,' he announced. 'You won't shoot me in the back. As long as I steer clear of guns, you're helpless.'

The statement might have rung true had the keen hearing of Kid Cheyenne not detected a muffled sound coming from the bowl of the top hat pressed to Ken Martin's bosom.

It was the unmistakable sound of a derringer being cocked. Martin took two more steps towards the bright sunlight and then swung on his expensive shoe leather with the tiny weapon in his hand.

The interior of the church resounded as flashes of venomous lead filled the air with gunsmoke.

Martin had fired his solitary shot at the tall gunman but only succeeded in taking a chunk out of the wooden pulpit beside Kid Cheyenne. The ruthless hired gun glanced at the pulpit and then swiftly drew both his six-shooters and returned fire.

Both his bullets cut through the silk vest and knocked Martin off his feet. Martin had been dead before his bulk had landed on the floorboards.

Kid Cheyenne walked to where Martin lay and stared down at the lifeless man as smoke trailed up from the two neatly placed bullet holes in his vest. He had no questions in his mind. He did not care who this man was or had been. He did not give a damn why he had been hired to kill him.

He had earned his money and that was all that mattered to the notorious gunman. His side of the murderous bargain had been fulfilled.

The Kid twirled the guns on his fingers and then holstered them both in one unified action. He stepped over the body just as Martin's right arm fell to its side and the small derringer slid across the boards.

He stared at the small gun as smoke trailed up from its barrel and then smiled at the body.

'It takes a bigger gun than that to kill me,' he sighed.

Kid Cheyenne pulled the brim of his black hat down to shield his eyes and strode out into the blazing sunlight. He descended the steps and walked back along the wide street to where he had left his mount.

ONE

Waco stood like a glittering jewel in an otherwise barren landscape. The town was expanding at an alarming rate as the factories from the eastern seaboard started to replenish the newly conquered section of the Wild West. The hired gunman raised himself in his stirrups and guided his black quarter horse down a slight rise, then headed straight at the massive town.

Kid Cheyenne needed provisions and Waco was the best place in a thousand miles to get them. He held his long leathers between the fingers of his left hand and steadily approached the normally peaceful settlement.

The horseman watched every single building as he entered the outskirts of the town. He had never experienced any type of trouble since he had made Waco his base but his honed instincts told him that could change at any time.

Few of Waco's citizens knew what the mysterious Kid Cheyenne did for a living and that suited the hired killer just fine. He eased back on his reins and looped a leg over the head of his sturdy mount. He slid to the sand and then led the lathered up animal into the livery stable. The blacksmith touched his sweating brow and began removing the hefty saddle and bags off the back of the exhausted animal.

'You staying in town long this time, Kid?' the large man asked as he steered the horse to a trough and allowed it to quench its thirst.

Kid Cheyenne rested his backbone against one of the stable's tall barn doors and shrugged.

'That depends, Wally,' he replied.

Wally Depp had been a blacksmith for twenty years and yet he had never encountered anyone quite like the tall figure. He rested the saddle on a bench and then handed the saddle-bags to the Kid.

'Depends on what exactly?' he probed.

Kid Cheyenne looked from under his wide black hat brim at the far meatier man and sighed. A wry grin etched his hardened features as he slung the bags over his shoulder.

'In my line of work you never know when someone will send for you and require your services, Wally,' he explained vaguely.

Depp rested his massive knuckles on his hips and moved closer to the hired killer. He eyed the Kid up and down a few times and then looked straight at the man with the expensive shooting rig strapped around his hips.

'And what kind of work do you do, Kid?' the black-smith grinned. He knew that whatever it was the

14

younger man actually did for a living, he would never reveal it.

The smile turned into a wide grin as Kid Cheyenne pulled out a few silver coins and dropped them into the apron pocket of the blacksmith.

'That should cover it,' he said as he forced himself away from the barn door and started walking toward the red brick buildings that denoted the start of the large town.

Kid Cheyenne walked for nearly a half mile before he came to a three-storey building. He paused at the entrance and looked at the array of high chimneys dotted across skyline. Smoke billowed out of each and every one of them as they pumped out their own brand of pollution into the air.

The smell of beer brewing and other less appealing aromas filled his nostrils. He knew that less than a couple of blocks from where he rested, a vast army of men laboured in factories making the things that were essential even in the wildest of western regions.

This was civilization, he thought.

He shook his head and turned to open the metal mailbox on the wall. His was the fifth box. He inserted a key and then opened it, pulled out the solitary telegraph message and pocketed the small envelope.

The walk to his small office took less than a minute for the notorious gunman. He opened the door and was greeted by dust that was so thick you could almost chew it. He crossed the office, which consisted of a small desk, a chair and a cot, and opened the sash window. The air from outside was little better than the dust but at least it cleared the room enough for the Kid to see from one side to the other.

The Kid placed his saddle-bags on the desk and sat down on the swivel chair. He knew that civilization would one day make people like himself extinct but not quite yet. As he rested on the chair, he pulled the envelope out of his pocket and opened it. The message was brief, as all such wires tended to be. Few men who wanted to hire the deadly services of a hired killer cared to risk putting their own necks in a noose.

The message read:

Kid Cheyenne. Come to Bloodstone.
Have a job for you.
Signed Ben Black.

The Kid rubbed his dusty jaw and then got back to his feet as he moved to the wall calendar and studied it. He knew that Bloodstone was a remote town set in the middle of a desert that somehow had managed to defy the elements and prosper where others had become ghost towns.

'If I set out tomorrow I should be able to get there in about eight days,' he told himself before turning on his heels and returning to his bags. His fingers unbuckled one of the satchels and pulled out a wad of notes. He grinned and pushed the money into his inside breast pocket, then checked his holstered guns.

The Kid knew that this might be blood money and he had killed Ken Martin to earn it but it was better than doing what most folks were forced to do in Waco.

16

At least he did not have to sell his soul to the various factory owners.

'Reckon I'll go bank this,' he mumbled before leaving his office and marching back out into the street. The further he walked into the heart of Waco, the dimmer the sky got as clouds of black smoke hung over the industrious settlement.

He banked the money and strode back out into the main street, rubbing his unshaven jawline as he gathered his thoughts. He was thirsty and ready to indulge in emptying a bottle of whiskey down into his craw as he crossed the wide street. The Palace saloon had the prettiest bargirls in all of Waco and that was where he was headed.

The traffic on the road was busier than usual. Wagons and buckboards wove around horsemen and buggies. He reached the opposite side of the street and had just hopped up on to the sidewalk when something alerted his finely tuned instincts.

The Kid stopped, rested a hand on a metal porch upright and turned around. For most men it might have been impossible to spot anyone clearly in the crowded thoroughfare but not for Kid Cheyenne.

He pulled the brim of his Stetson down to shield his narrowed eyes and then spotted the five men moving amid the hundreds of others. There was something different about them.

Unlike every other person on the street, they were looking in his direction. Most might have thought that nobody could have ever spotted them in an ocean of ever-moving bodies, but they would have been wrong.

17

The sense of survival had sharpened like a straight razor in the hired killer's guts. He had never doubted or even questioned that gut feeling when it alerted him to danger.

Kid Cheyenne turned away from the men across the busy street as though he had not seen the five men who were watching his every move. He rested a shoulder against the upright and stared at the saloon window. The reflection told him where they were and what they were doing.

He rubbed his jaw again.

This was the first time that he had ever encountered trouble in Waco. For two years, this had been a safe haven for the gunslinger.

'Howdy, Kid,' a female voice caught his attention from the open doorway of the Palace saloon. 'You look a mite troubled. Why don't you come on in and let me soothe that fevered brow of yours?'

Kid Cheyenne glanced at the bargirl. He gave a nod of his head and took the three steps to her side. He looked down on her barely contained heaving bosom and recalled the last time he had seen it in all its powdered glory.

'You see them five varmints across the street, Ellie?' he asked without turning.

She squinted across the street and then shrugged.

'There must be close to a thousand folks on the street and most of them are men, Kid,' she purred before toying temptingly with the tails of his bandanna. 'Why don't you come on in and let me rub that trail dust off your face?'

18

'Later,' Kid Cheyenne placed a finger under her chin, tilted it up and then planted a kiss on her bright red lips. He smiled and then turned and stared back at the crowd. He caught sight of the five men resting their backs against the bank wall as they continued to watch him.

'Is that a promise, Kid?' she cooed as he stepped away from her and looked to both sides of the long sidewalk.

'You bet it is,' he touched the brim of his hat and winked before marching into the crowd. Within seconds she could no longer see the mysterious man as he moved deeper into the dozens of people.

Kid Cheyenne only slowed his pace long enough to check that the five men were trailing him on the opposite side of the street. He was right, he thought.

They were following him.

His mind raced with every step as he mingled with the townsfolk. He tried to figure out who they could be yet no matter how hard he tried, his mind refused to recall ever seeing them before.

The Kid slid into an alley.

Any normal man might have been scared but not the stone-faced Kid Cheyenne. He had tackled more than five gun-toting hombres before he eventually had realized how fast he was with his guns and decided to hire his skills out to anyone willing to pay his price.

Yet he wondered who these men were and why seeing him had sparked their interest. Then over the heads of the townsfolk who continued to pass along the street he caught a glimpse of the five men again as they snaked along the opposite side of the street.

He could see the anger in their faces.

They had lost sight of the hired gunman and were desperately trying to find him again. Kid Cheyenne grinned and then pushed his way through the passing people. He stepped off the sidewalk behind a heavily laden wagon and moved to the edge of the vehicle's tailgate.

His eyes never left their backs as they carried on their futile search. He waited for a few buggies to pass and then hastily ran across the street until he was on the sidewalk directly behind the five men.

Now he was following them.

TWO

Kid Cheyenne must have walked for more than a mile following the five heavily armed men. They seemed oblivious to the fact that the man they were vainly trying to trail was now walking in their wake with his hands resting on his holstered guns. Without missing a step, Kid Cheyenne flicked the leather safety loops off his matching pair of .45s.

The confused men paused for a moment at a corner and then scattered in five directions. The Kid stopped and inhaled deeply as he wondered what they were planning. Thoughtfully, he pulled out a cigar from his inside pocket, placed it between his teeth and bit off its end.

The Kid spat at the sand, then produced a match and ignited it with his thumbnail. He cupped the flame and raised it to the end of the cigar and puffed a few times before tossing the blackened splinter at the street.

He was looking straight ahead but the five figures had vanished from view into the crowd. Kid Cheyenne blew a long line of smoke at the ground and shook his head.

This was getting a tad tiresome, he thought.

He pushed the tails of his coat over his holsters so that his guns were exposed to every passing eye that passed. With his lungs filled with the toxic smoke, the Kid started to walk once more. His eyes darted at every face before him as he cautiously reached the corner where the five men had scattered from.

There was an alleyway to his left.

At first he only gave it a brief glance and was about to turn his back when he heard noises coming from the shadows that stretched up between the nearest buildings. Kid Cheyenne took a step backward and then spotted a figure pushing his way toward him through the men and women going about their daily rituals.

Kid Cheyenne did not recognize the face that came closer to his tall lean frame as he chewed on the flavoursome cigar and studied the man. He knew that he was one of the five who had spotted him only a few moments earlier, though.

The man stopped about three feet from the hired gunman and looked him up and down. Just like the Kid, he kept his hand resting upon his gun grip.

'Are you the hombre they call Kid Cheyenne?' he asked nervously as his eyes kept glancing up into the alley.

The Kid gave a silent nod.

The man moved closer to the infamous hired killer. He was scared and unable to hide the fact from his observer as he pointed into the alley.

'I've bin told to bring you to a critter who wants to hire you, mister,' he stammered as he jabbed at the air. 'He got himself a place on the east side of town.'

'What you pointing into this alley for?' Kid Cheyenne asked through a cloud of smoke.

The man cleared his throat.

'That's the quickest way to his place,' he lied. 'He told me to bring you there without folks getting wise to the fact that he was hiring you. This alleyway leads straight to his place.'

Kid Cheyenne gave a nod.

He could smell a trap and this one was ripe.

'This *hombre* got himself a name?' the Kid asked as he stepped down beside the unknown man.

'I don't know it. He just paid me to find you and bring him to his house,' the man muttered as his brain strained to try and think of a story that the hired killer might believe. 'Are you coming with me or not?'

The tall gunslinger frowned and withdrew the cigar from his lips, then studied its blackened tip. The Kid returned the spent cigar to his lips, dipped his long fingers into his vest pocket and pulled out a fresh match. He scratched his thumbnail across its brightly coloured end. The match erupted into flame and was raised to the cigar as Kid Cheyenne continued to look at the nervous messenger.

'Are you coming or what?' the man snapped.

Kid Cheyenne slowly puffed. He lowered the match and flicked it away as smoke hung in a cloud beneath the wide brim of his black Stetson.

'What's wrong?' the Kid asked as his eyes reverted to the alley and narrowed. 'You look a little troubled.'

The ruffled man rubbed his neck and kicked at the sand as he moved closer to the alley. He glanced over his shoulder at the deadly gunman.

'I'm going to tell the hombre that wants to hire you that you don't seem interested,' he bluffed. 'I don't give a damn whether you go there or not. I've bin paid anyway.'

Kid Cheyenne reached out, grabbed the bandanna of the messenger and dragged him back. He twisted the stained cloth until their eyes met. A wicked smile carved a route across his face as he watched the man's eyes begin to bulge in their sockets.

'I'm plumb weary of all your damn lies. Now tell me the truth,' he drawled. 'Who are you and the rest of your back-shooting pals?'

The man vainly scratched at the Kid's vice-like grip. He could not get the Kid to loosen his hold. He coughed and started to see stars dancing in his eyes.

'I . . . I can't breathe,' he croaked.

Kid Cheyenne loosened his grip slightly. 'Now spit it out. Who are you and what do you want of me?'

The messenger was blue as the Kid slammed his stinky frame against the nearest wall. A cloud of dust flew off the inept man as he attempted to drag his six-shooter from its holster.

Kid Cheyenne drew one of his own guns and cracked its steel barrel across the wrist of his unwilling victim. As blood poured from the gash on his wrist the man felt the gun pressed into his guts. The sound of the hammer being cocked widened the hapless man's eyes even wider than when he was being choked.

'OK, don't shoot,' he stammered as the Kid pressed the barrel of his .45 deeper into his belly. 'I'll tell you.'

'I'm listening,' the Kid whispered into his ear.

The man inhaled deeply as he felt the heat of the cigar's glowing tip hear his face. He blinked hard and then started to reveal what was going on.

'Jeb Carver and his kinfolk are hidden in the alley waiting for you to follow me down there,' he said.

Cheyenne tilted his head. 'That name sounds kinda familiar.'

'It should,' the terrified messenger muttered. 'You gunned down his brother Rufe two months back. They've bin hunting you to get revenge.'

The eyes of Kid Cheyenne tightened.

'What are you to this Carver varmint?' he asked.

'My name's Joe Smith. I work for him,' he said. 'He pays my wages. I do as I'm told and that brung me here with him and his kin.'

Kid Cheyenne pulled the cigar from his teeth and rammed it into the mouth of the trembling man.

'Suck on that while I try to figure this out,' he snarled like a caged cougar.

Smith puffed frantically as if each draw on the smoke would be his last. He was shaking from head to toe as his far taller companion considered his options.

The Kid pulled Smith away from the wall and turned him to face the shadowy alleyway. He rested a hand on the shoulder of the shaking man and leaned close to him as he pushed the barrel of his six-shooter into the man's backbone.

'If you play your cards right, Joe,' the Kid said, 'You'll be alive when this is over. If you get smart, I'll kill you. Savvy?'

'I savvy.'

'Start walking.'

The fearful man was still puffing like a locomotive on the cigar. His sweat-soaked spine felt the gun encourage him to start walking. Smith entered the alley with the Kid a stride behind him.

The sun could not reach the depths of the alley. Black shadows marked both sides of it as they protruded from every corner and overflowing garbage pails. A strange blueish hue made it difficult to focus clearly on anything abandoned within its confines.

Yet even hampered by the half-light, Kid Cheyenne could see clearly. His honed eyesight searched the depths of the alley as he and Smith slowly walked deeper into it.

They had journeyed for more than fifty feet into the aromatic shadows when Smith started to run forward screaming at the top of his voice.

'Shoot him, boys,' Smith yelled at the top of his voice as he stumbled and then swung around on his heels and fumbled for his gun. 'I brung him like you wanted.'

Kid Cheyenne had been surprised by Smith's sudden display of courage and stopped in his tracks. He glared at the pathetic figure as Smith managed to pull his six-gun from its holster and started to cock its hammer.

For a few moments as they had started into the shadowy alleyway, Kid Cheyenne had considered sparing the inept Smith. But as the barrel of his gun left its holster, the deadly hired gunman changed his mind.

Without uttering a word, the Kid squeezed on his trigger.

The confines of the alley echoed to the deafening sound that spewed from his six-shooter. The blinding light lit up the alley for a mere heartbeat as he sent a bullet towards the yelling gunman.

Smith suddenly fell silent as the deadly accurate bullet tore through his chest. The gun fell from his hand as Joe Smith buckled. Even in the dim illumination of the alley Kid Cheyenne could see the blood explode from the neat bullet hole in Smith's chest. Before the lifeless figure had landed on his back, the four other heavily armed members of the Carver clan emerged from their hiding places with their guns cocked and ready.

The Kid looked through his smoking .45 at them.

'Quick, shoot the skunk, boys,' Jeb Carver shouted at his cousins. 'He's already done for Joe. Kill him.'

The Carver boys did not require telling twice. Within seconds the entire length of the alley was filled with the choking smoke of their weaponry. Bullets ricocheted off the brick walls as Kid Cheyenne stood firm and drew his other lethal six-shooter.

Even with bullets whizzing past his lean frame he did not flinch as he cocked the hammers of his weapons. It was near impossible for either the Carvers or the Kid to see one another through the dense gunsmoke but, unlike his ambushers, the Kid was no stranger to being the target of avenging kin.

Although Kid Cheyenne could not see the four men who were blasting their guns, he could see the blinding flashes of their .45s in the swirling smoke.

He fired his six-shooters at the flashes. Within seconds the Kid had heard the groans of two of the closest of the gang as his lethal bullets finished them off and they fell to the ground.

Suddenly he felt the heat of the Carvers' bullets as they passed within inches of his face. The Kid strode forward at an incredible pace. Each step was marked by a bullet exploding from his guns to either side of the narrow confines.

'Kid Cheyenne don't die that easy,' he shouted.

Suddenly he sensed that his remaining foes were to either side of him. Without even aiming he instinctively turned the barrels of both his Peacemakers and fired the final bullets into them. The bushwhackers squealed like stuck hogs and crashed through the gun smoke. One man hit the ground face first at the Kid's feet as the other somehow staggered away from his hiding place and hovered less than a yard from where the hired gunman stood.

Kid Cheyenne shook the spent casings from his guns as his eyes studied the dying man before him. Blood was visibly pumping crimson gore from three holes in Jeb Carver.

There was no emotion in the ice-cold features of Kid Cheyenne as he started to reload his guns. His eyes darted down to the .45 still gripped in Carver's bloody hand and then returned to the face of the shaking bushwhacker.

'You gonna use that gun?' he asked Carver.

Blood trickled from the lips of the older man as his thumb pulled back on his gun's hammer. The sound of the hammer locking into position filled the alleyway.

'I'm gonna kill you,' Carver growled like a wounded bear and then raised his trembling hand. 'Kill you for killing my brother.'

Kid Cheyenne snapped his gun chambers and cocked both his hammers again. He tilted his .45s and then fired into the chest of the bushwhacker. The bullets ripped through the muscular Carver and sent his bloodied body backwards. Craver crashed into the alley wall and then slid to the ground. His gun fell from his limp hand as the Kid loomed over his prostrate form.

Kid Cheyenne holstered his smoking guns and spat. He turned and walked back to the bright main street. He felt no satisfaction killing the five men he had left in the alleyway for one reason.

He detested killing anyone without being paid to do it.

THREE

The main street appeared to be different to when Kid Cheyenne had walked along it only minutes earlier. Now the crowd had scattered like stampeding steers after hearing the gut-wrenching sound of gunfire. The Kid walked calmly along the now empty thoroughfare as a handful of Waco peace officers ran toward him in a frantic search for the origin of the devilish gunplay.

Chet Brent, the captain of the Waco police force, skidded to a halt beside the tall hired gunman. As sweat poured down his pale face, he eyed the Kid as he tried desperately to get his second wind.

'Did you hear them shots?' Brent asked the stony-faced gunman. 'You got any notion where they come from?'

The Kid shook his head slowly as he carefully watched the rest of the lawmen gather just behind Brent's back. He rubbed his jaw and looked around the street.

'I thought it was thunder and lightning, captain,' he said as Brent managed to straighten back up. 'Looks like a storm's brewing by them clouds.'

Brent pushed his brown derby off his furrowed brow.

'Lightning?' he repeated as his men all stared up at the smoke-filled clouds as though trying to spot any activity in the heavens. 'That was gunfire.'

Kid Cheyenne shrugged and raised his eyebrows.

'Gunfire?' he muttered. 'Hell, I could have sworn it was thunder but you're more experienced at such matters than me captain.'

'Your damn right,' Brent gave a sharp nod of his head. 'I've bin a lawman for ten years and if there's one thing that I know for certain it's a gun being fired.'

The Kid watched as the lawmen squinted against the brilliant sunshine as they all tried to work out where the volley of shots had come from.

Brent frowned and pointed along the street.

'I reckon the shots must have come from down there someplace, boys,' he reasoned and waved his arm at his men. 'Come on, let's go investigate down yonder.'

The lawmen started running again, keeping just one stride behind their leader. The Kid exhaled and pulled the brim of his black Stetson down to cover his eyes as he continued on his way back to his office.

Kid Cheyenne had barely travelled fifty yards when he heard the distinctive voice of Brent booming out hysterically behind his wide back. The Waco lawmen had discovered the dead men and were making a real ruckus.

The deadly killer had never used his lethal skills in

Waco before and he grew anxious and crossed the street as scores of townsfolk suddenly reappeared and started to rush down to where the lawmen were shouting at the top of their voices.

The Kid rested a hand on an upright as he watched the men, women and even children practically racing to feed their curiosity.

He then turned and marched toward the livery stable.

As he entered the cool interior of the large structure, Wally Depp looked up from his anvil and paused from hammering a horseshoe. He rested his large hammer down upon the anvil and smiled at the hired gunman.

'I sure didn't expect to see you again so soon,' he stated as he walked toward the tall hired killer. 'I figured you was going to have yourself a shave, a bath and change your trail gear, Kid.'

'Change of plan, Wally,' Kid Cheyenne said as he glanced out at the street at the people who were still racing past the livery stable. 'I'll need my horse readied.'

The blacksmith stopped in his tracks and looked at the tall man before him. He tilted his head and rubbed the sweat off his face with a huge hand.

'I only just rubbed the critter down and give him a ration of oats, Kid,' Depp said. 'You intending taking that horse out again before he's rested up?'

Kid Cheyenne nodded and looked at his black quarter horse in the end stall. He turned to Depp and shrugged.

'I've got to get to Bloodstone,' he said.

'What's the hurry?' the blacksmith questioned. 'You should get some rest yourself and wait until tomorrow.'

Kid Cheyenne sighed. 'I can't help that, Wally. I've gotta ride out of Waco right now.'

The blacksmith tilted back on his heels and stared at the mysterious hired gunman. He had guessed long ago that Kid Cheyenne was far more than just another ordinary citizen of the busy town. No ordinary man sported a matched pair of pristine six-shooters unless they made their living with them. He started to nod knowingly as he swung his generous proportions around and started to walk towards the quarter horse.

'Did you have anything to do with that shooting I heard a few minutes ago, Kid?' Depp asked as he reached the stall and started to lead the black horse out into the middle of the livery stable.

Kid Cheyenne smiled.

'Why would you ask such a question?' he whispered.

'Maybe I'm just a nosy old galoot,' Depp stopped the horse and ran his large hands over its exhausted body. 'Well, did you?'

The Kid strode to the side of the blacksmith and then stopped. He did not look at Depp but concentrated on the dirt floor as he spoke.

'Five *hombres* decided to bushwhack me, Wally,' he revealed without turning. 'They wanted to kill me. I had to snuff out their candles.'

Depp grunted. 'I figured as much but why did they attempt to kill you?'

33

The Kid walked around the sturdy quarter horse and patted its neck as he drew closer to the blacksmith. He looked Depp straight in the eyes.

'They were the Carver family,' he started. 'I killed the leader of their clan a while back so they decided to avenge that simple deed.'

Depp scratched his unshaven chin.

'If they're dead,' the blacksmith mused. 'Why are you so all fired up? How come you wanna leave Waco right now?'

Kid Cheyenne pealed his coat away from his chest and pulled out a long cigar from his inside pocket and bit off its tip. He placed the cigar between his teeth and then found a match and struck it into life with his thumbnail. The flame flickered as he raised it to the end of the long cigar. He puffed and then blew out a line of smoke and extinguished the dancing flame.

'Captain Brent practically bumped into me as I was walking away from where I left the Carvers,' he informed.

'Chet Brent is as dumb as a three-legged mule,' Depp said as he watched the hired killer. 'Don't go fretting about him or his so-called law officers.'

'I've bin hired by some hombre in Bloodstone,' the Kid said and inhaled smoke. 'I figure it's best I get out of town until them bodies are buried. When my business there is finished I'll return here.'

Depp knew that it was pointless trying to dissuade his companion from leaving Waco. He walked back to the stall and dragged a dry blanket off a wooden rail. He returned to the horse and threw the blanket on the back of the quarter horse and patted it down.

'Don't ride this nag too hard,' he warned the Kid. 'He's so tuckered he's likely to bust a leg.'

Kid Cheyenne nodded as he screwed his eyes up and squinted at the wide open barn doors. Then, as the blacksmith plucked his saddle off a bale of hay, the tall gunman noticed the shadow of a man trace a route across the stable floor as someone approached the entrance.

Depp tossed the saddle on to the back of the quarter horse as Captain Brent marched into the massive livery. The blacksmith straightened up and watched as Kid Cheyenne pushed the tails of his coat over his holstered gun grips.

'Easy, Kid,' he said.

FOUR

The lawman came to an abrupt halt when he noticed the familiar sight of Kid Cheyenne. He frowned and walked towards both men as they stood beside the quarter horse. Chet Brent was not the brightest candle in the box but the Kid knew that even a dumb lawman was dangerous. Brent moved up to the nose of the horse and stroked it as he watched the muscular black-smith reach below the animal and pull its cinch strap toward him.

'Didn't I bump into you on main street, stranger?' he asked the gunman.

The Kid gave a silent nod of his head, then moved away to a stall and plucked his saddle rope and canteen off a stained wooden plank. He strolled back to the horse and secured both to the saddle-horn.

Brent edged closer to the heavily armed Kid.

'We found five bodies in an alley,' he stated, as Kid Cheyenne puffed on his cigar. 'Strange that you didn't hear the shooting and thought it was thunder.'

The Kid's eyes darted to the lawman.

'I still think it sounded like thunder, Captain,' he said dryly through a cloud of smoke. 'It sure didn't sound like shooting to me.'

Captain Brent took a backward step and studied the lean man more carefully than he had done earlier. He cleared his throat when he spotted the nickel-plated guns in their hand tooled holsters.

'What is it you do exactly?' he asked cautiously.

'I'm a drummer,' Kid Cheyenne lied as he rested both his hands on his gun grips and glared at the lawman. 'I travel around taking orders for guns. Pistols mostly, like these beauties.'

Brent bit his lip.

'They sure are a fine pair of .45s,' he stated. 'Can I have me a closer look at one of them?'

The blacksmith caught the eye of the Kid over the bowl of the saddle. Kid Cheyenne poked the brim of his hat off his brow and took a step toward the lawman.

'You wanna take a look at one of my guns, captain?' he drawled ominously.

Brent nodded and held his hand out.

'I sure do, son,' he confirmed. 'I'm never seen such a shooting rig in all my days.'

Faster than either the lawman or Depp had ever seen anyone drag a six-shooter from its holster, the Kid drew one of his .45s from his left holster and held it out.

'Anything to oblige, captain,' Kid Cheyenne said as Brent took hold of the Colt.

'Man, you sure are quick on the draw,' Brent

gulped as he studied the six-gun. He then raised the barrel to his nose and sniffed. 'This gun smells like its bin fired recently. Why would that be, stranger?'

'It has,' The Kid said. 'I was practising with both my guns this morning before I rode into Waco.'

'Are you leaving Waco so soon?' Brent nervously handed the gun back to its owner and watched as the hired gunman expertly twirled the weapon and then dropped it into his holster.

'I've a client who wants to place an order and in my business it don't pay to keep folks waiting,' the tall man said through cigar smoke. 'You understand.'

Chet Brent nodded firmly as Depp handed the Kid his long leathers. Both men watched as Kid Cheyenne mounted the quarter horse in one fluid movement. He steadied the horse as his eyes burned into the lawman.

'I'll be seeing you, Wally,' said Kid Cheyenne from the corner of his mouth, then eased his reins to his left and tapped his spurs into the flanks of the sturdy animal.

'Don't you go tuckering that horse, Kid,' Depp said as he and the law officer watched the horse and rider slowly exit the livery stable.

Captain Brent rubbed his neck thoughtfully and turned to the blacksmith. He trailed the larger man to where a blackened coffee pot rested on the red hot coals of the forge.

'You wanna cup of this brew, Chet?' Depp asked.

With a baffled expression on his face, Brent nodded and then returned his attention to the large barn doors. He shook his head and then looked at the blacksmith.

'Who in tarnation is that hombre, Wally?' he asked as a hot tin cup was handed to him. 'He sure don't look like any drummer I've ever seen before.'

Depp sipped his coffee. 'He ain't selling the things that most drummers deal in, Chet. I reckon it takes a certain breed of drummer to deal in what he does.'

The lawman held his cup in his hands and frowned through the steam that rose into his face. He started to nod as another thought filled his mind.

'I got me a notion that critter ain't exactly what he says he is, Wally,' the captain announced before taking a gulp of the hot beverage.

The blacksmith masked the grin on his face with his large hands and then stared at his weathered boots.

'You're a genius, Chet,' he cackled. 'Pure genius.'

FIVE

The sprawling settlement known as Bloodstone nestled at the foot of an arid mountainous mesa and marked the end of what most drifters called civilization. Whatever lay beyond the towering scarlet monolith out on the vast scorched desert was unknown to most who travelled this way. Some said that only the Devil knew exactly what perils the arid terrain had hidden within the shimmering heat haze.

Others regaled that Satan himself had created the desolate desert to resemble his fiery home, for the Lord could never have envisaged such a horrific place. Whatever the truth, the murderous heat of the red rich desert bathed the large town in unholy waves of barely endurable heat.

It was an unlikely land for anything apart from venomous vipers to even consider inhabiting, yet the remote settlement had defied the odds and done just that.

Bloodstone had flourished. Yet it might never have grown roots and survived had it not been for the crystal clear water that continually flowed from the ground at the foot of the imposing mesa.

It had created a virtual oasis amid the otherwise satanic terrain; a virtual flower in an otherwise barren cauldron of merciless heat. It seemed odd that the Lord would have provided such a gift and yet have it come from what could only be described as the very bowels of Hell itself.

Yet none of the grateful recipients who quenched their thirst had even given a second thought to the cold water's origins. To them it was a gift, and one that they would never question.

It was a precious bounty that defied the elements and never ceased carving a route through the town that had grown to either side of the sparkling stream, ending its journey just outside the unmarked boundaries of Bloodstone, where it formed into a sparkling lake.

The lake provided enough water to supply not only the townsfolk of Bloodstone but also the herds of three cattle ranches that had sprouted up in the desolate land that surrounded the remote town. The sparse vegetation offered little sustenance to either man or beast but vital supplies brought in regularly by weekly wagon trains kept every living creature well nourished.

Bloodstone had defied the odds and flourished where most of its contemporaries had become forgotten ghost towns, yet beneath the surface of this tranquil place, trouble was brewing within the confines of its boundaries.

In every town ever created by the hands of men, greed had eventually raised its ugly head. For years since its first permanent structure had been erected, Bloodstone had been a quiet place where the troubles of the outside world had passed the townsfolk by.

Yet during the previous few months, something had changed.

Various cowpunchers from the trio of cattle ranches that shared the arid plain had been mysteriously killed but so far none of the outfits had claimed responsibility for the murderous outrages.

Greed had been just the beginning but then grown into something far more dangerous. Killings had been virtually unknown until recently. A hatred grew like a cancer in and around Bloodstone. It festered like an open wound and eventually engulfed every single person in and around the sprawling settlement. For the first time in the history of the remote cattle town, a war was brewing and yet so far none of the ranchers had managed to gain a telling advantage.

The town's ultimate fate was balanced on a knife edge.

It would take very little to tip the scales and the men at the heart of the unrest knew that only too well. Yet one of their number was ready and willing to tip the scales in his favour and that was why Ben Black had sent the telegraph wire to the notorious character known only as Kid Cheyenne.

SIX

Countless lurid thoughts infested the fertile imagination of the horseman as he carefully steered his weary quarter horse deeper into the desert towards the remote settlement known as Bloodstone. He wondered why anyone would want to hire his infamous skills in this devilish region. As sweat trailed down from beneath his black Stetson, he began to also wonder who Ben Black actually was and why he needed someone killed.

The Kid glanced all around his mount as darkness began to sweep across the heavens and replace the cloudless blue sky with bright points of light.

Twilight had always troubled the deadly Kid Cheyenne for he knew only too well that was when the most dangerous of creatures emerged from their lairs. The small hairs on the nape of his neck started to tingle as his eyes narrowed on the high mesas above him. The canyon between the mountainous monoliths was steep on both sides and led someplace, he thought.

He threw his long leg over his cantle and dis-mounted the sorrowful quarter horse in one fluid action, carefully studying the strange land he found himself in.

In his haste he had not chosen the longer route to his chosen destination but mistakenly imagined it would be far faster to cross the rugged terrain instead. Few if any men had ever taken this precarious trail to Bloodstone and he now knew why.

He studied the fading landscape for a hint that he was on the right course but there was nothing to reas-sure the hired gunman. The Kid rubbed his jaw as he removed his hat and laid it down before the tired horse. He filled its black bowl with water from one of his canteens and as his mount quenched its thirst he took a sip of the precious liquid and then returned the stopper to its neck.

Bloodstone had to be near by now, he kept telling himself but why would anybody build a town out here in a blistering desert? After the previous few days and the men he had dispatched to their Maker, Kid Cheyenne was now anxious.

He hated killing anyone without being paid and so far he had lost count of how many free deaths he had added to his brutal tally.

'Bloodstone must be close,' he heard himself mutter as he started to notice a telltale glowing in the distant sky between the mesas. 'I got me a notion that's the town's lights yonder, horse.'

The black raised its head with water dripping from its chin as its master plucked the Stetson off the ground and placed it on his head. Darkness in the desert came swiftly and everything was transforming before the Kid's very eyes.

'We'd best keep going,' he told the quarter horse as he poked a boot toe back into the stirrup and eased his lean frame back on to the saddle. He gathered up his loose leathers and tapped his heels into the flanks of the exhausted animal. 'I figure we're close and I sure don't intend spending another night out here.'

The words had barely left his lips when he heard the sound of a coyote howling to his left. His eyes darted to where the sound still echoed off the rocks and encouraged the lone horseman to increase his mount's pace.

Kid Cheyenne was a man who seldom showed any hint of being afraid when confronted by any amount of gunmen but being out in the darkness in the middle of the desert was different. He jabbed his spurs again and started his mount trotting across the stony ground.

Normally he would never push his prized black mount this way but Kid Cheyenne knew the seemingly innocent rocks were far more dangerous than the places where they normally rode. Deadly snakes combined with wolves, coyotes and mountain lions made it far safer to keep moving. They had already passed the bleached bones of numerous animals in the rocky desert and it was Kid Cheyenne's intention not to add to their number.

As the horse carefully negotiated a route through

the gigantic rocks that flanked him, the Kid caught a fragrance that alerted his weary senses.

It was the scent of water.

SEVEN

The one thing that was worth more than golden nuggets in the merciless desert was water. It alone provided life in an otherwise arid terrain and everyone who had ever ridden into the depths of the unforgiving parched deserts scattered across the Wild West knew that simple fact. The horseman encouraged his mount to follow its nose as the black quarter horse defied its own exhaustion as it too sensed what its master knew was close.

The horse carefully crossed over the rubble that had fallen from both sides of the high mesas. Neither the rider nor his mount could actually see where the water flowed from the ancient springs but they could smell and hear it.

Kid Cheyenne sat motionless atop his sturdy horse as it practically dashed to the constant sound of bubbling water that came from the base of one of the mesas.

The quarter horse reached the starlit spring and dropped its head into the fast-flowing cold stream. For a few moments the horseman just sat and observed everything around him. The sky was like black velvet with jewels pinned to it. They bathed everything in the rocky area in an eerie hue, which did nothing to ease the trepidation that continued to nag at the lean hired killer.

He unhooked his canteens and then dismounted.

As his horse continued to drink, he removed their stoppers and carefully lowered them into the icy water. The Kid looked at the groove cut into the rocks, which he surmised must have taken countless years to achieve due to the incessant flowing of the precious liquid.

The Kid held both his canteens by their leather straps as they slowly filled with water. He turned to where he had first noticed the glowing sky far below their high vantage point.

So that was Bloodstone, he thought.

The settlement had been constructed around the waterway as it coursed through the otherwise arid terrain. Even by starlight, it was an impressive sight.

As he hauled the full canteens from the water and secured their stoppers, his eyes noticed the moon hanging low in the star-studded sky.

He returned the wet canteens to his saddle-horn and then pulled a fresh cigar out of his jacket's breast pocket. The Kid bit off the slim cigar tip and spat the leaf at the ground before placing it between his teeth and scratching a match with his thumbnail. As it exploded into flame his eyes darted around his rocky surroundings before raising the flame upward and sucking in the smoke. A few puffs and he tossed the blackened splinter of wood aside before picking up his long leathers and slowly encouraging his quarter horse away from the icy water.

'You've had enough, horse,' he said as he reached up and placed the palm of his hand on the saddle-horn before stepping in his stirrup.

He mounted the muscular animal in one fluid motion and then gathered up his reins. Bloodstone looked nothing as he had imagined it.

Although its buildings glowed in the comforting amber light of countless street lanterns, the gunman still felt uneasy.

There were some towns that had that effect on the Kid. He seemed unable to accept that most folks were unlike himself and had no desire to kill, even for money.

For years he had imagined that everyone had a secret agenda to kill him. He mistrusted each and every single one of them just in case they were planning to unleash their hidden guns on him and shoot.

Kid Cheyenne tapped his boots against the sides of his loyal mount and started to descend down toward Bloodstone. As the horse carefully navigated a safe route through the massive boulders, he wondered who his paymaster was.

He had a name but that told him nothing.

Who, he wondered, was this Ben Black?

And who did he want killed?

For the first time in his life, the Kid pondered another deeper question. It was one that he had never even considered before.

Who did Ben Black want killed, and why?

As the black quarter horse headed steadily through the growing darkness toward the glowing lights, its master found himself battling something he had never even imagined he had dwelling in the dark recesses of his deadly mind.

He was battling with his conscience.

EIGHT

As moonlight flashed across the countless horns of the grazing steers gathered around the large lake just beyond Bloodstone there was no hint of the trouble that was fermenting in the ranch houses of the three individuals who owned them.

The three cattle spreads had tolerated one another's presence in and around Bloodstone for more than a decade but finally the rivalry had turned into something far more dangerous.

Envy and greed now festered and had been growing like a cancer for months. The three men who controlled the individual cattle spreads resented sharing the sparse vegetation around the lake. Now one of them had decided to take the law into his own hands and fulfil his ambitions.

Rancher Ben Black had already started his devilish plan rolling by sending his men out on the range to kill his rivals' hired cowboys.

The unrest had grown to lethal levels. Cowboys

51

from each of the ranches were suddenly being tar-geted and killed. For years most of the cowpunchers had not even been armed but now it seemed that every single one of them was wearing a brand new six-gun and carried a repeating rifle next to their saddle rope. Yet these were not gunslingers who toted the growing arsenal of firepower. They were just ordinary cowboys who seldom used six-shooters for anything apart from firing at the clouds to scare off marauding packs of hungry wolves.

Although Ben Black denied that he was behind the mayhem, he had long harboured a desire to be the only rancher in Bloodstone and therefore become the wealthiest cattle rancher in the territory.

Out of the three ranches, Black's Lazy B spread was the newest and by far the smallest of the trio. In his mind the only way he would achieve his ambition was to take control of its neighbours. Yet neither Casey O'Hara of the Double C or Toke York of the Twisted Bar were willing to talk business.

Ben Black had purchased the Lazy B only a few years earlier and his fellow ranchers considered him to be nothing more than an upstart who would prob-ably go the way of his predecessor.

Neither O'Hara nor York realized exactly how badly Black wanted to control all of the region's steers. Even the deaths of their cowhands had been dismissed at first as accidents.

Good men have a tendency to judge everyone by their own standards and as neither York nor O'Hara would even consider doing such a barbaric thing as having simple cowpunchers killed, they had found it impossible to fathom that anyone else would be so underhand.

Yet Ben Black was a man who had stooped far lower in the past than just having his cowboys kill his rival's men. Black had a long history of doing things that most would find unimaginable. To him, there were no rules and he had always gotten what he wanted no matter what it cost.

That was exactly how he had obtained the Lazy B.

NINE

The moonlit expanse beyond the lantern light that washed out from every structure within the sprawling Bloodstone looked somehow unreal to the horseman, who carefully guided his exhausted mount down the steep mesa. The eerie illumination gave everything an almost deathly hue. Only the brightness of the rising moon and the already twinkling stars cast any actual light upon the lake and its lush range before the desert and its lifeless expanse. The horseman squinted hard at the flat terrain beyond the fertile ground near the lake. He had never seen anything quite like it and that troubled the lone rider.

Few men had travelled the entire territory but Kid Cheyenne had covered most of it. His travels had taken him to practically every inch of the large territory, from its snow-covered peaks to its most arid of deserts.

Yet this was the first time he had ever ventured to this unholy landscape. As the Kid tapped his spurs gently into the flesh of his weary mount in a bid to keep the animal moving, he felt uneasy.

Kid Cheyenne had never seen another place like Bloodstone.

It seemed to defy logic and made no sense to the infamous Kid. The blistering desert heat still dragged sweat from his body even though it was night. Most places, no matter how hot they got during the day, grew cooler after sundown. Why was this cauldron different?

The question tormented him. He rubbed his bandanna tails over his hardened features and continued to glare out at the strange landscape. He had heard many tall tales concerning Bloodstone over the years and maybe that was why he had managed to avoid it until now.

Some stories said that the Devil himself had created this land and punished the unwary for entering its unmarked borders. Apart from the spring of icy cold water that trailed from the foot of one of the mesas, the Kid began to believe that this place could only have been made by Satan.

It resembled the bowels of Hell and yet there was a town standing a few hundred yards before the black quarter horse. He could not understand why any sane folks would even consider living in this inferno.

Then the sound of the countless steers drew his attention.

Kid Cheyenne glanced up and stared at the animated herd of long horns, which bayed at the moon like wolves as they grazed on the plentiful vegetation near the lake. He pushed his black hat off his brow and watched them as the horse reached level ground. Then he concentrated on the array of buildings that flanked the stream as it cut a course to where it accumulated at the lake.

He noted silently that most of the buildings he was approaching were constructed from brick. That seemed odd to the Kid for men tended to only use brick when they intended to remain for a long time.

Bloodstone was no temporary settlement, he mused. However, he could not fathom why anyone would choose to remain in such a place.

A wooden marker with the single word painted upon its weathered surface stood close to the outermost edge of the scattering of structures.

'Bloodstone.' The Kid read the name bathed in moonlight aloud as his mount passed it. 'At least this is the right place, horse.'

The horse's hoofs neared the fast-flowing stream. He straightened up on his saddle and stared at the numerous store fronts. Their lamp light spilled out on to the hardened sandy street he was negotiating.

Scores of men filled its boardwalks to both sides of the thoroughfare as the quarter horse slowly entered the street and was caught in the light that spilled across the lathered up animal.

Kid Cheyenne pushed his coat tails over his holstered .45s and carefully studied the unknown surroundings. The hired killer felt beads of sweat trailing down his face as he carefully studied each of the store front façades.

A hundred sets of curious eyes were watching his

arrival in town. It made the horseman anxious as his quarter horse moved slowly through the amber light.

When Kid Cheyenne was anxious, he was even more dangerous.

TEN

The tally of dead cowboys now stood at four. A sizable chunk of the three ranches' wranglers, and yet none of the assassinated men worked for the Lazy B. The fear of becoming the assassin's next target was bearing down on the simple cowpunchers and making them increasingly nervous. Some had already quit and headed to safer pastures but those who remained were growing more and more tense as they feared the next bullet would have their name on it.

So far the Double C had lost three of its finest cow-punchers and the Twisted Bar had its top wrangler mysteriously shot in the Golden Spur saloon only two nights earlier. There were never any witnesses to the bloody outrages, leaving the ranch owners of both the Twisted Bar and Double C outfits totally confused by what was happening.

All ranchers Casey O'Hara and Toke York knew for certain was that none of their rival Ben Black's cowhands had suffered the same fate. It seemed out of the question that Black could be behind the killings, yet the more they thought about it, the more it started to make sense.

Having a gut feeling was one thing but it was not proof and that gnawed at both O'Hara and York. They had armed their own cowboys but knew that none of their trusty cowboys were gunmen. They were just ordinary cattlemen and even just wearing their brand new shooting rigs did not make them any safer.

There was a war brewing in Bloodstone. They had heard of similar outbreaks of violence in other parts of the ever-expanding territories but had never imagined that it would ever raise its ugly head in their part of the country.

Both the ranchers knew that their hired hands were on the brink of following the other cowhands and leaving Bloodstone for safer pickings. None of them wanted to end up like the four who had already been murdered.

Sixty-year-old Casey O'Hara had more steers than his rivals and was a quiet man who seldom left the confines of his ranch house. Toke York on the other hand was even older yet still rode with his cowhands during their regular checks of their grazing herd. His herd was about half the size of O'Hara's and mixed freely with all three of the ranches' stock that shared the fertile range and lake.

Ben Black however was unlike either of his fellow ranch owners. He had arrived in the area with a handful of heavily armed men and within a matter of months had somehow managed to get control of the Lazy B. At the time few questioned what had actually happened to his predecessor but as the tension grew and the tally of dead cowboys mounted, a lot of people were starting to wonder exactly who Ben Black was.

At the time of Black taking control of the Lazy B, very few people in or around Bloodstone gave a second thought to the sudden departure of its previous owner. They had accepted Ben Black's word that the old rancher and his cowboys had simply left Bloodstone one night never to be seen again.

Now with the growing tally of deaths, it seemed that everyone was growing suspicious. Although the Lazy B was by far the smallest of the three cattle ranches and had only about a quarter of the livestock Black's competitors had, he was openly ambitious and had attempted to buy out both O'Hara and York.

Neither of the older ranchers had been tempted by Black's initial offers and originally laughed off his attempts to buy them out.

Yet Black was not discouraged or dismissed quite so easily.

His greed far outweighed any other consideration. The mysterious owner of the Lazy B decided to change his approach and decided that if he could not buy his rivals' ranches, he would obtain them in a far more brutal way.

That was the reason Ben Black had sent for the renowned hired killer Kid Cheyenne. He wanted both York and O'Hara gunned down by the most lethal exponent of the fast draw. Black knew that even though it was very expensive to hire the Kid, he was also well aware that it was far cheaper than buying both the Double C and Twisted Bar.

Even if the ranch owners had agreed to sell their lucrative spreads to the upstart, Black had no intension of actually paying them.

The unscrupulous Black had never paid for anything if he could get it by killing. That was why he had originally turned up in Bloodstone with his gang of equally ruthless gunmen. Black and his gang had conned and slaughtered their way across the territory and reaped the financial rewards before reaching the remote settlement.

Ben Black had learned about the three cattle spreads who regularly brought their combined herds to Dodge City. The plan to take control of the trio of ranches had festered in his evil mind long before his arrival in Bloodstone.

Even as he had sent the telegraph message to the mysterious Kid Cheyenne, Black's devious brain was calculating how he and his gang could kill the hired gunman without paying him for gunning down York and O'Hara.

To the unscrupulous Black it seemed a perfect way to not only take control of all three of the cattle ranches but also save the enormous fee that he knew Kid Cheyenne would charge for fulfilling his lethal contract.

It was only five days since Black had sent the wire to Kid Cheyenne in Waco and he had never expected that, due to unforeseen circumstances, the hired gunman would arrive so soon and already be riding into Bloodstone.

Black would soon learn that it did not pay to under-estimate the man known only as Kid Cheyenne. All those who had done so in the past were now buried deep in graveyards across the wilds of the vast terri-tory.

Neither of the normally easy-going ranchers, Casey O'Hara or Toke York could truly accept that some men were truly evil and would do anything to get what they wanted. Yet Ben Black was driven by an insatiable appetite and had never shunned away from spilling blood to get it. His naïve rivals on the range were like moths fluttering around a bright flame to the dark-hearted Black. They were standing in his way and he had no scruples about swatting them.

Yet Black was about to be taught a lesson.

He had made the fundamental error of sending for the most dangerous creature ever to suck in air with the intention of having him kill his rivals and then kill him as well. It was a plan doomed to failure simply because Kid Cheyenne was no ordinary hired gunman.

In all of his numerous gunfights the Kid had mirac-ulously never even been wounded. Some said that he led a charmed life because he was the Devil's spawn. Others dared not utter his name aloud for fear that some unholy force might overhear their utterances.

Whatever the truth actually was, the one thing that was correct about Kid Cheyenne was that he was the fastest gunman ever to travel through the untamed territory.

Unknown to Ben Black, he had opened Pandora's box.

ELEVEN

Kid Cheyenne was getting a little unsettled as he steered his weary black mount along the main street. His eyes darted to every curious observer huddled beneath the numerous store front overhangs. Each of the folks flanking the lean horseman had one combined thought filling their minds. Who was this stranger and why had he ridden through the gruelling desert and crossed between the mountainous mesas to reach Bloodstone?

The trail road had been used by wagon and stagecoaches alike for years and provided a safe way in and out of the remote settlement, and yet this high-riding stranger had chosen to take the most perilous of routes.

Why?

There seemed no logic to it.

The Kid sniffed the air and then spotted the livery stable bathed in the amber lantern light that spilled out from its large interior. He eased the black to its left and held his long leathers firmly as the sturdy animal jumped across the fast-flowing water that streamed down the centre of the street. The horse steadied itself and then continued on towards the open barn doors.

The rider patted the neck of the horse as it slowly neared the livery. His squinting eyes focused on the towering wooden structure and for the first time in hours he began to relax.

'You done good, horse,' he whispered as his mount halted and snorted at the sand. 'There were times back there in them rocks when I was starting to figure we'd never find this godforsaken town.'

Kid Cheyenne looped his right leg over the bowed head of the quarter horse and slid to the dust soil. The Kid tugged on his long leathers and got his tired mount's attention. The quarter horse raised its head and glanced at its master as lantern light splashed over both of them. They were six feet from the bright interior of the cathedral-like edifice but the Kid was still cautious as he swung on his heels and studied the eyes that were still studying him.

'Folks around here sure are nosy, horse,' he muttered. 'I don't like being the centre of attraction. Anybody would think that they ain't ever seen somebody riding into Bloodstone before.'

His narrowed eyes surveyed the high-sided structure for a moment before he walked into the livery stable with the horse in tow. The Kid was like a cautious wild cat as his eyes darted around the interior of the wooden building.

'You looking to stable that sorrowful black horse, mister?'

The strange voice came from across the livery as a greasy man strode out of the shadowy corner towards him with a long-handled hammer resting on his shoulder. The Kid gave a silent nod as he studied every visible inch of the stable. He noted there were exactly eleven horses in various stalls and room for five more.

'Anybody would think that nobody ever visited these parts by the way so many folks were eyeing me and the nag out there, stranger,' the Kid sighed wearily.

'I was up in the loft when you rode down out from the mountains, stranger,' the large figure informed. 'That was the first time I ever seen anyone enter Bloodstone from that direction. Reckon folks are just plumb curious.'

The Kid wiped the dust off his brow with the back of his sleeve and shrugged. 'It was the shortest trail here from Waco.'

'You looking to stable this nag?' the liveryman repeated his question. 'I figure he's about exhausted.'

'That was the notion,' Kid Cheyenne replied.

The liveryman walked past the dust-caked Kid and did not slow his pace until he reached the forge. He rested the long-handed hammer against the forge and then turned back to face the Kid.

'For how long?' the big man enquired.

'I ain't sure.' The Kid fished a few silver coins from his vest pocket and dropped them into the palm of the sweat-covered man. 'Will that cover it for a few days?'

The liveryman nodded as he pocketed the coins. He shook his muscular neck and sweat droplets glistened as they flew off his head. He took the long leathers from the Kid and led the black horse to the middle of the vast interior.

The Kid watched as the liveryman, who was called Mort Favour, started to remove the saddle from the steaming horse. It seemed that the blacksmith had muscles that the hired killer had never even seen before. They flexed as he tossed the saddle on to a bale of hay as though it was a feather.

'You got business in town?' the man asked, even though he already knew the answer.

'You could say that,' Kid Cheyenne answered drily.

'I know most folks by sight but I can't recall ever seeing you before,' Favour added as he carefully inspected the lathered up horse.

'I've never bin here before,' Kid Cheyenne replied as he moved closer to the busy liveryman. He was amazed at the speed with which Favour went about his duties. Steam rose off the back of the quarter horse when its blanket was peeled off its sweat-covered back. 'I doubt that I'll ever come back here once my business is done.'

The large man eyed up the Kid.

'By the look of them handsome guns of yours,' he stated as he tossed the blanket over a bench, 'I'd say you ain't a drummer selling cough mixture.'

The Kid almost smiled as he warmed his aching bones before the hot coals in the forge. 'I'm no drummer.'

'I figured that,' the big man lifted a bucket of warm water off the forge and carried it back to the waiting horse. He pulled out a large cloth from the bucket and started to wash the suds off the horse's coat. 'The last time I seen such a fine belt and holsters was when one of the Lazy B boys come in here looking to have his mount shod.'

The statement intrigued the Kid. He narrowed his eyes as they stared hard at the busy blacksmith. His head tilted to the side.

'A cowboy wearing a fancy shooting rig similar to mine?' he queried. 'That don't sound normal.'

Favour paused for brief moment. 'That's what I was thinking, stranger. Cowboys ain't got no call to wear fancy gun-belts and holsters, but this one was. First time I ever seen a cowpuncher who looked more like a gunslinger.'

'Maybe that's what he was,' the Kid said.

Favour grunted with a nod. 'I've seen hundreds of cowpokes and most ain't even armed apart from a folding knife in their back pocket. That *hombre* was no cowpuncher.'

The Kid edged closer to the blacksmith.

'The Lazy B ranch, you say?' he repeated.

'That's what I said.' Favour strangled the large cloth and continued wiping the horse down. 'What does a simple cowboy want with a fancy gun-belt?'

'That's kinda strange,' Kid Cheyenne agreed.

Favour looked through the rising steam of the soaking wet horse and raised his eyebrows. 'Four cowboys bin gunned down in the last month or so. It's getting mighty dangerous out there for regular cow-punchers.'

'What do you mean by regular cowpunchers?'

Mort Favour again paused his work. 'I mean real cowboys, stranger. Some of the varmints around here ain't exactly what they claim to be.'

'Like the *hombre* from the Lazy B?' the Kid pressed.

'Exactly,' the blacksmith winked. 'I've bin here for nearly twenty years and I've never seen any real cowpoke dressed like some of the Lazy B boys are. They ain't what they're pretending to be. I can't figure it.'

Kid Cheyenne pulled a cigar from his pocket and bit off its tip thoughtfully. He spat at the forge and then scratched a match and cupped its flame. He raised it to the cigar and started puffing, before tossing the spent match on to the coals.

'Things are getting really weird around here,' Favour added as he massaged the horse's legs with his powerful hands. 'A cowboy got murdered in a saloon the other day.'

Kid Cheyenne raised an eyebrow. 'So all the killings ain't all bin out there on the range?'

'Nope,' the liveryman nodded. 'Somebody has now started to bump folks off in the very heart of Bloodstone.'

The Kid sucked on smoke and brooded. What had seemed to be a simple job to the experienced hired gun was now taking on a whole new aspect. He pulled the cigar from his mouth and glanced at the busy Favour.

'Tell me something,' he drawled as cigar smoke drifted from his mouth and hung under the brim of his Stetson. 'Who owns the Lazy B?'

Mort Favour paused his toil and looked straight at the gunman. The expression carved into his weathered features seemed to visibly drain of colour.

'Why that'd be a certain Ben Black,' he stated. 'He's a real unpleasant critter like all the men he got working for him. Black says that he owns the ranch but not one single person in Bloodstone ever seen the last owner of the Lazy B leave the area.'

'That's kinda suspicious,' the Kid said thoughtfully.

Favour grunted in agreement. 'Ain't a single varmint in Bloodstone got the guts to tackle Black about that. Even the sheriff is so scared of Black that he just shakes his damn head and shrugs if you talk to him about the Lazy B.'

'And you say that you doubt that any of them boys he got working for him are real cowboys?' The Kid rubbed his jawline and returned the cigar to his mouth.

The blacksmith took hold of the loose reins and backed the quarter horse into a stall. He hung a feed bag over the animal's nose and then turned and stared at the Kid.

'How come you're so interested, stranger?' he asked.

Kid Cheyenne blew smoke at the floor and eyed the burly figure as he moved across the livery toward him. Favour scratched his neck and stood before the gunman.

'I'm just a curious soul,' the Kid drawled.

'It don't pay to get too curious in this town lately.' Favour seemed to be warning the Kid about the perils that had taken over the once peaceful Bloodstone. 'Folks around here are darn scared of meeting the same end as the cowboys. The other ranchers have started arming their boys and there ain't nothing more dangerous than a cowpuncher with a loaded gun.'

Kid Cheyenne lowered his arms and rested his hands on his holstered .45s. A smile etched his thoughtful face as he raised an eyebrow.

'I ain't the breed of critter to panic, friend,' he stated firmly. 'Folks that try to creep up on me usually find that out pretty fast.'

Favour looked at his companion and sighed.

'Are you a gunslinger?' he asked.

'I'm just a drummer,' the Kid said through another cloud of cigar smoke before adding ominously. 'I sell plots in cemeteries.'

The liveryman grinned from ear to ear at his quietly spoken companion. He shuffled his feet and then cleared his throat.

'My name's Mort,' Favour announced. 'What do they call you?'

The lean gunman grinned. He never told anyone his true name and seldom even revealed the identity that most folks knew him by.

'Most folks just call me Kid,' he replied.

Favour rested his knuckles on his broad black belt and watched as Kid Cheyenne turned and strolled out of the livery stable and into the street. He rubbed his neck thoughtfully and shook his head.

'Kid what?' he wondered.

TWELVE

The news of the stranger's arrival in Bloodstone did not take long to reach the ranch house of the Lazy B. Riding as if his life depended upon it, hired gunman Hank Smith whipped his mount mercilessly and thundered across the arid terrain toward his paymaster's stronghold. Like the other ranches on the range, the Lazy B had no physical boundaries yet was set on the most fertile soil in the area. Smith rode like a man possessed toward the wooden structure. The horse galloped up to the long structure and did not slow its pace until the very last moment. Smith dragged rein just outside the building, leapt from his saddle and ran hurriedly to the ranch house entrance.

He burst into the Lazy B Ranch house and frantically looked around its main room until he spied Ben Black sitting before a roaring fire. He pushed his way between the rest of the gunmen and stood panting like a hound dog above the seated Black.

'He's here, Ben,' Smith told Black. 'That varmint you wired is in Bloodstone right now.'

A mutual gasp went around the rest of the heavily armed men as they closed in around the sweat-soaked Smith. None of them had imagined that the famed Kid Cheyenne would arrive so quickly, and that troubled them.

'You gotta be loco, Hank,' Jake Cooper dismissed and poured himself another glass of rye, chuckling. 'The Kid couldn't have gotten here so fast. Not unless he flew here.'

'He's here, I tell you,' Smith argued with a shaking fist. 'I seen the critter down at the livery.'

Laughter filled the room. It only stopped when Black raised his voice and boomed out at the other hired guns.

'Shut the hell up,' Black ordered.

Black turned and watched his fearful hireling as he stood sweating above his chair. Black rose to his feet and grabbed hold of Smith's trembling shoulders. He shook Smith hard until the breathless man finally calmed down.

'Are you sure?' Black snarled.

Hank Smith stared straight into the face of his humourless paymaster and glanced at the door, which was still rocking on its hinges.

'Kid Cheyenne is in town, Ben,' Smith stammered. 'He just rode into Bloodstone. He's here, I tell you.'

Black released his grip and paced thoughtfully around the nervous gunman as he considered the fact more intently. His mind raced as it was filled with dozens of thoughts concerning the infamous hired gunslinger that he had sent for in a moment of drunken bravado. It was an action that, once he had sobered up, Black had instantly regretted.

But the message had already been dispatched.

'How'd you know it was him, Hank?' he asked as he walked across the room to the door and gazed out across the lake to the array of amber lights that sparkled like precious jewels across Bloodstone.

Smith moved through his fellow hired guns to the side of the frowning Black and jabbed at the dark air with his index finger. 'I seen him riding into town. He came from the mesas like a phantom. It was him, I tell you.'

Black viciously grabbed hold of Smith's bandanna and dragged the shaking man close to him. His eyes burned into the younger man.

'Did you hear anyone call him by name?'

'Not exactly,' Smith admitted. 'But he had these two ivory-gripped guns poking out from his hips. That was a professional shooting rig, Ben. It was Kid Cheyenne, I tell you. Who else could it be?'

'Yeah, who else could it be?' Black released his grip and then turned to face his other men. He was confused and it showed as he moved back across the room to a whiskey bottle. He filled a glass with the fiery liquid and then downed it in one throw. As the whiskey burned a trail into his innards, Black looked at his hired men.

'I got me a feeling that one of our rivals might have done exactly the same thing as we did,' Black considered through gritted teeth. 'Either York or O'Hara could have sent for a hired killer just like we done.'

Cooper stared across the room at the troubled Black.

'That's right, Ben,' he drawled. 'That would explain how this gunslinger has arrived in Bloodstone so fast. York and O'Hara could have wired for someone days before you telegraphed Kid Cheyenne.'

The expression on Black's hardened features seemed to pale as he refilled his whiskey glass and stared at its amber contents.

'Do you really think them galoots got the guts to hire a gunfighter to come after me?' he asked his gang. 'I know that I done it but would they? Neither O'Hara nor York are fighting folks like us. I can't imagine they'd even want to hire some hombre to do their killing for them.'

Smith shook his head and stared across the lamp-lit room at the others. He moved closer to Black.

'Them ranchers and their boys ain't used to handling guns and maybe they figured that the only way to save their bacon was to bring in a varmint that could,' he suggested.

'Yeah, you could be right, Hank,' Black's eyes darted at Smith. He started to nod his head in agreement before looking at the rest of his gang in turn.

'You saw this galoot ride into Bloodstone from the mesas?' Cooper probed his fellow hireling. 'That's mighty strange and no mistake.'

Smith ran his fingers down his whiskers. 'If that fella is Kid Cheyenne and he came straight from Waco, the mesas are in the right direction.'

'It would explain how he got here so damn fast

though, boys,' Black mused. 'But there are a lot of other towns in that direction and he could be any of a half dozen hired guns.'

The oldest of the gathered gunmen was a forty-year old man called Billy Kane. He had been listening to the vibrant conversation carefully from a hardback chair set in the corner. He rose to his feet and walked across the floorboards toward Black, who was still staring at the whiskey full glass in his hand.

'I got me a notion, Ben,' Kane said before he picked the whiskey bottle and poured himself three fingers of the fiery liquor. He sipped it and then locked eyes with his boss. 'Why don't we head on into Bloodstone and find out exactly who that varmint is? Seems a tad pointless us just gabbing here like a herd of womenfolk.'

Black grinned. 'You could be right, Billy.'

Jake Cooper was still not convinced that the stranger in town was the infamous Kid Cheyenne. He sighed heavily.

'Kid Cheyenne couldn't be here yet, could he?' he asked the gathering. 'I've heard that the Kid is so busy killing folks for the highest bidder that he has a waiting list.'

'Whoever this critter is,' Black said as he downed the whiskey and placed his empty tumbler next to the bottle, 'we're gonna go and find out. Billy is right, there ain't no profit in just gabbing like a bunch of old hens. We're going to town to find out.'

'I'll go saddle the horses,' one of the men said, before heading toward the door.

'I'll give you a hand,' Smith said and trailed his cohort out into the darkness. Both men headed to the shelter where they kept their horses.

Black glanced at Kane. 'You bring my pinto here, Billy.'

'OK, Ben.' Kane grabbed his Stetson, pulled it over his mop of grey hair and strode on after his fellow gunmen.

Black was still not convinced that the stranger might not be the very man that he had telegraphed but could not reason the speed that Kid Cheyenne took to reach Bloodstone.

'Even Kid Cheyenne couldn't have travelled all the way from Waco to Bloodstone that fast,' he muttered, before biting his lip and turning to face his gunmen. 'Is that even possible?'

'I've never ridden that trail myself but a lot of the old-timers reckon it's a real fast way to travel, Ben,' one of the gunmen said as he too walked from the ranch house.

Black rubbed his thumb knuckle into his jaw. He plucked his gun-belt off the table, swung it around his hips and buckled it up. He leaned over and secured the leather laces that hung from the two holsters to his thighs.

He drew each gun in turn and checked they were fully loaded before dragging his hat off a stand and placing over his black hair.

'Let's go and see if this is Kid Cheyenne,' he muttered to himself before closing the door behind his broad back and standing beneath the porch overhang.

Within a matter of only moments, the men began leading saddled horses from the shelter to his right and moving towards the front of the ranch house.

Billy Kane tossed the long leathers to Black, who immediately stepped into his stirrup and mounted his excitable horse. Black gathered up his reins as his men mounted.

'Ready, boys?' the infamous Ben Black asked his hired men.

The riders all gave out a guttural groan as they held their mounts in check. Following Black's lead, they spurred their horses hard.

A cloud of dust rose into the star-filled heavens as the six riders galloped towards the glistening lights of Bloodstone.

THIRTEEN

Toke York was a wily old-timer who had been one of the first to discover the small oasis set amid the merciless terrain and had two hundred prime steers under his Twisted Bar brand. Even though he had the second largest herd, York had only three cowhands left after having one of his men mysteriously murdered only days earlier. Shortly after learning that Casey O'Hara had lost three cowhands in relatively quick succession, his own younger cowhands had fled. Now York had only three cowpunchers remaining and even though he had provided them with guns for protection, he was well aware that they could quit at any time.

Revenge was now the only thing keeping the aged Twisted Bar cowhands in Bloodstone. They wanted just a chance at discovering the culprits behind the recent slaughter. York's old cowhands were like their boss, they were a stubborn bunch and unwilling to try and find a new place to live and work. The thought of dishing out their own brand of justice was the only thing keeping them at the Twisted Bar.

Yet even the determined old-timer Toke York was well aware that his men were no match for the skilled gunmen who now frequented the range in the guise of being ordinary cowboys. It was only a matter of time before the snipers' bullets found the four remaining Twisted Bar cowhands, and York knew it.

Like his fellow rancher, Casey O'Hara of the Double C, he was now desperate to have the killing stopped while there were still cowboys on the range.

But York and O'Hara were good men. They had no idea how to stop the ruthless killings. To them, it was totally alien to even think of trying to use any form of violence to obtain what you desired.

Only bad men with blackened hearts did that.

Every fibre of O'Hara's and York's beings knew that their neighbour Ben Black was behind the bloody outrages but neither could prove anything. It was one thing to know in your guts that only your hired cowhands were being slain and your rival had not had any of his men harmed, but proving it was impossible.

Had either of the ranchers done the unimaginable and sent for a hired gunslinger to kill Black and his gang members? The thought tormented Black as he led the horsemen and drove their mounts through the grazing steers toward Bloodstone.

To all who knew York and O'Hara it was totally out of character but not to Ben Black or any of his gang of deadly hirelings. They considered that everyone was as unscrupulous as they were.

Ben Black raised himself up in his stirrups as he led

his riders around the rim of the vast lake and thundered on toward Bloodstone at a perilous pace.

To the sound of hoofs echoing off the surrounding structures, Black galloped ahead of his men into the main street of Bloodstone. The knowing eyes of the townsfolk watched from the well-illuminated store fronts as the six riders guided their horses toward the towering livery stable.

With a cloud of dust floating up into the star-filled sky, the Lazy B horsemen hauled back on their long leathers and stopped their mounts outside the wide open barn doors.

Black dismounted and strode with his hands on his holstered guns. He did not slow his pace until he entered the heart of the stable and looked around until his vicious eyes located Mort Favour.

'Get over here, Favour,' Black growled.

Favour rose to his feet from an upturned barrel and pushed the strands of limp hair off his face. His face was like the man himself and full of muscular twitches.

'What do you want, Black?' the blacksmith grunted as he rested his corn cob pipe down on the edge of the forge and started to stroll towards the owner of the Lazy B.

Black heard the sound of spurs behind him as two of his men followed him into the livery stable and stood a few feet behind their boss. Black clenched both his fists and shadow-punched the air between him and Favour.

'Listen up, Favour,' Black snarled angrily. 'You had yourself a customer in here a short while back. I wanna know who he was and where he's gone. Savvy?'

The liveryman was unimpressed by any of the men who faced him, even though they were heavily armed and he had nothing to defend himself with apart from muscular courage.

'You talking to me, Black?' Favour asked as he advanced from the forge toward the three men.

Black was taken back by the huge man, who seemed to have no fear in his large body. He took a step backward and dropped his hands on his gun grips.

'Back off, Favour,' Black growled.

The liveryman halted his progress and stared at the far smaller man. A smile covered his face.

'The young varmint who was in here didn't tell me his name, Black,' Favour grunted as he pointed at the stalls full of horses. 'He just left his horse in here but he didn't tell me where he was headed.'

Black frowned.

'He must have told you who he was,' he reasoned.

Favour shook his head. 'I asked him all right but he just said folks call him Kid.'

The face of Ben Black lit up.

'Kid?' he repeated.

'Yep,' Favour nodded. 'That's all he said. I asked him but he didn't seem to wanna tell me anything else.'

Black turned to his men and marched out of the livery stable to their horses and the rest of the mounted men. Black rested his hands on the bowl of his saddle and glanced to each and every one of them.

'I reckon young Hank was right, boys,' he said

before stepping in his stirrup and then hauling himself back on to his saddle. 'That stranger must be Kid Cheyenne.'

Billy Kane steered his horse toward his boss.

'Are we headed back, Ben?' he asked. 'I figure this critter might not be too friendly if we go looking for him.'

Black swung his horse around, stared into the well-lit street and pointed at the closest saloon.

'I got me a notion that if we head on up to the Spinning Wheel saloon we might find Kid Cheyenne there, boys,' he said, before getting his pinto moving with a kick of his heels. 'C'mon.'

Kane looked to Cody Carson next to him and shrugged.

'This might just be a really bad notion, Cody,' he whispered to his fellow gunman.

Both horsemen got their mounts moving and followed the rest of the Lazy B riders through the spilling store lights on towards the saloon. Of the six heavily armed men, only Ben Black seemed to be unaware of the risk anyone took by approaching the man known only as Kid Cheyenne.

FOURTEEN

The six Lazy B horsemen moved through the amber
lantern light, turned and lined their mounts up
before the long twisted hitching pole outside the
Spinning Wheel saloon. At that very moment Casey
O'Hara and his friend Toke York moved from out of
the hardware store and stopped in their tracks. Both
ranchers were in Bloodstone with a few of their
cowhands to purchase provisions for their mutual
ranches.

O'Hara raised a hand and stopped his friend's
progress down from the high boardwalk to the awaiting wagon. The flatbed vehicle was laden with bags of
flour and numerous other things that both ranches
regularly purchased from the store.

York looked at O'Hara and was about to ask why he
had been prevented from descending to the street
when he noticed the curious expression on his pal's
face.

'You look like you just seen a ghost, Casey,' York
said before he too stared in the direction that O'Hara

was looking. As he squinted through the eerie illumination and starlit street, he noticed Black and his gang dismounting opposite.

York swallowed hard and moved behind one of the store's porch uprights. His eyes flashed back and forth between the saloon and his friend.

'What do you reckon they're doing in Bloodstone, Toke?' O'Hara finally managed to say. 'I've never seen the whole bunch of them away from the Lazy B before.'

York exhaled and shook his head. 'Beats me, Casey.'

Had either man been younger they might have succumbed to their first instinct and temptation. Both the ranchers wanted to do what they knew they were no longer capable of doing any longer. Yet even if they had been younger, they would have stood little chance against men who obviously knew how to handle their weaponry.

Men cut from the same cloth as Black and his gang never used their fists when they could easily kill with their guns. O'Hara did not seem to breathe until he had seen Black and his men dismount and enter the Spinning Wheel.

He turned to York after they had lost sight of the men beyond the swinging saloon doors and rested a hand on the older man's shoulder.

'We'd best get these provisions back to our ranchers, Toke,' he suggested drily. 'With them varmints in the saloon we'll have no trouble getting back home.'

York rubbed his dry mouth.

'I thought we was going to get us a drink before we

headed home, Casey,' he said.

'That's what I was thinking before I seen them varmints,' O'Hara rubbed his sweating face and pointed at his top wrangler. 'Get the wagon ready, we're headed home.'

York looked disappointed.

'I've bin a lot of things in my life, Casey,' he said. 'But I ain't never bin a coward. I'm thirsty and I'm gonna get me a drink.'

Casey O'Hara shrugged and then nodded reluctantly. He turned back to his three cowhands and then walked down the steps toward the wagon.

'Leave two saddle horses for me and Toke,' he told the waiting cowboys. 'You three can head on back to the range and deliver the goods to the Twisted Bar and then store the rest of the goods in our store house.'

The cowboys mounted the wagon and cracked its hefty reins down across the sturdy horses between its traces. The heavy vehicle slowly moved away from the hardware store and began the slow journey to their ranches.

Casey O'Hara looked over his shoulder at Toke York as the elderly rancher descended to the sandy street.

'Satisfied?' O'Hara asked his friend.

'Nope,' York grinned impishly. 'I'm still thirsty.'

'There are three saloons in town,' O'Hara said. 'Which one do you wanna have a drink in, Toke?'

The flickering amber light caught York's face and highlighted the twinkle in the older rancher's eyes. He did not answer as he walked across the sand towards the Spinning Wheel saloon and stepped up on its boardwalk.

The sound of a boisterous out of tune piano being hammered into submission inside the saloon filled their ears.

As York's hand rested upon the top of the saloon swing doors he felt his friend's hand fall upon his shoulder. York turned and looked up into the concerned O'Hara's face.

'What's wrong, Casey?' York asked innocently. 'We're just going in to get us a drink.'

Against his better judgement, O'Hara released his grip and followed his friend into the noisy saloon. He knew that his impish friend had a habit of stepping on folks' toes and just prayed that he did not try to antagonise either Ben Black or any of his equally dangerous gang.

FIFTEEN

The saloon was full to overflowing as York and O'Hara entered the large interior. The sound of bad piano playing grew louder but was mostly drowned out by the raised voices of countless townsfolk in various stages of drunkenness. The larger O'Hara could smell the scent of the saloon's bargirls but for the life of him he had no idea where they might be in the crowded room.

Tobacco smoke hung about four feet above the sawdust-littered floorboards and made even the Double C rancher's eyes start to water. He placed a firm hand on Toke York's shoulder and turned his friend.

'This ain't a good idea, Toke,' O'Hara repeated his concern and gestured with a jerk of his head for them to find another saloon. Toke York had no desire to leave the popular watering hall because his flared nostrils had located the fragrant aroma of hard liquor.

'Quit fretting, Casey,' York patted the rancher on his shirt front. 'We're only in here to quench our thirst.'

'There's a few other saloons in town that we could do that in, Toke,' O'Hara reasoned. 'And every damn one of them is safer than this 'un.'

'C'mon, Casey,' York pinched his friend's cheek and started to chuckle as he turned around and started to push his way through the wall of men between the bar counter and himself.

The sheer volume of human flesh filling the Spinning Wheel as they jostled for space in between the dozen or so card tables made it virtually impossible for anyone close to the bar counter to observe the ranchers as they made their way through the tobacco smoke.

Ben Black tossed a coin at one of the bartenders as a bottle of whiskey was placed on the damp surface he and his five gun-hands were leaning upon.

Black snatched one of the thimble glasses from the pyramid of identical drinking vessels and turned towards the closest table set against a wall. His gang copied their boss and each grabbed a glass as they eagerly moved to the table. They dragged hard chairs from every other table and assembled beside Black as he pulled the bottle's cork with his teeth.

Only Billy Kane remained standing as the rest of the gang sat down and started drinking. Kane had survived a score of bloody battles during his career as a gunman and had no intension of sitting with his back to the room. He pressed his spine against the torn and tattered wallpaper as his eyes surveyed the smoke-filled room through the fumes of his whiskey.

'Why don't you sit down, Billy?' Black growled as he

poured the strong liquor into his men's glasses.

'I'm looking,' Kane replied simply.

'Looking at what?' Carson laughed.

Kane spat at the sawdust without casting his eyes in his cohort's direction.

'I'm just looking,' he drawled before sipping at his whiskey thoughtfully. 'I'll let you know if I see any-thing worth talking about.'

Black and his seated gang roared with laughter. They continued drinking as all thoughts of finding the deadly Kid Cheyenne faded.

After what had seemed like an eternity, York and O'Hara reached the bar counter and managed to catch the eye of one of the bartenders. They were on the opposite side of the horse shoe-shaped counter and neither Black nor his gang spotted them. Men to either side of the ranchers swayed back and forth like ships about to sink. O'Hara had to use his bulk in order for them not to be crushed.

Two glasses were placed before them and swiftly filled with amber liquor by the bartender. Toke York grabbed the man's sleeve as his friend placed a golden coin down and flicked it at the bartender.

'Leave the bottle, sonny,' York winked and grabbed the clear glass bottle before downing his whiskey and then refilling his own thimble glass. 'Much obliged.'

O'Hara was getting tired battling with the other men propping up the counter as they continuously bumped into his back like a tidal wave.

He leaned closer to York and grabbed his arm.

'Let's try and find us a table and a couple of chairs,

91

Toke,' he suggested. 'I'm starting to feel like I just tangled with my prize bull.'

The ranchers cut a course through the crowd in search of a vacant place to rest their aching bones so they could enjoy their drinks. Both men got lucky as they neared the back wall of the Spinning Wheel. Two of the townsfolk, who looked as though they must have started drinking several hours earlier, shakily got to their feet and staggered away just as O'Hara and York reached the wall.

O'Hara physically forced York down on to a chair and then sat down himself. The owner of the Double C grabbed the bottle from his friend's hand and refilled his own glass.

'Wherever Black and his boys are,' O'Hara remarked as he downed his whiskey, 'I ain't seen them.'

York sniffed the air. 'I can smell females, Casey.'

O'Hara poured more whiskey into his glass and exhaled.

'Don't you start getting horny, Toke,' he growled. 'We're a tad too old for that kinda thing. Just drink your rye and keep your eyes open for trouble.'

Toke York frowned across the card table at his fellow rancher. He scratched his head as he filled his mouth with whiskey and swilled it around his gums. He swallowed and then held out his empty glass to be replenished.

'What kinda trouble would that be, Casey?' he asked.

O'Hara rolled his eyes.

'Black and his boys are in here someplace and I don't hanker to end up like our cowhands,' he said firmly.

'Quit fretting. Black is a yellow belly,' York whispered. 'Him and his gang of thugs never kill folks when there are witnesses, do they?'

'You're right,' O'Hara agreed.

'I figure we're safer in here than we are out on the range, Casey,' York grinned. 'Even if they spot us, I sure doubt they'll start shooting.'

Casey O'Hara nodded in agreement but still felt no easier in his mind. He kept looking at the crowd that surrounded them and filled his glass again.

'I know you're right but I'm still nervous, Toke,' he admitted before swallowing the fiery liquor. 'We both know that Black must be behind our cowpokes getting shot. I'm sick and tired of attending damn funerals. Every one of them boys I planted were younger than me.'

York nodded. 'I know what you mean, Casey.'

'When is it gonna end?'

'Damned if I know, son,' York sighed and tossed another shot of whiskey into his mouth. As it burned a trail down into his innards, he shook his head sadly. 'Damned if I wanna know.'

SIXTEEN

Contrary to what Ben Black had assumed, Kid Cheyenne had not quenched his thirst in the first saloon he came across after leaving his quarter horse at the livery stable an hour earlier. Although the journey from Waco had been tough, it was hunger rather than thirst that had driven the gunman as he had steered his rangy frame down the main street until he had located a small café. Finding it had been easy for Kid Cheyenne; he had just followed his nose and homed in on the fragrant aroma.

The Kid washed the remnants of his hearty meal down his throat with the last of his black coffee and patted the corners of his mouth with the tails of his bandanna.

'Would you like a refill, handsome?' the voluptuous female who was both cook and waitress in the tiny café asked as she picked up the plate that had been wiped clean with the last of the buttered bread.

He looked up at her and smiled.

'No thanks, ma'am,' he replied before sighing and

rubbing his thankful stomach. 'That was the finest meal I've had in many a day.'

She nearly blushed. 'Why thank you. I try my best.'

As he rose to his full impressive height she looked up into his chiselled features and fluttered her eyelashes at him. She moved away from the round table and allowed him to squeeze passed her. The half-dozen tables and numerous chairs did not provide a lot of room in the otherwise empty premises.

The Kid had brushed awkwardly against the soft-skinned female and they briefly looked at one another. He cleared his throat in embarrassment as she turned away from him.

Without even realizing it, the Kid watched her as she moved to the rear of the café and placed the plate and cutlery in a sink near the cooking range. As she turned to face him again, he quickly looked away.

'What's your name, stranger?' she asked as she wiped her hands on her apron and slowly negotiated a route between the tables back toward him.

'They just call me Kid,' he replied and plucked his dust-covered Stetson off the hat rack on the wall. He stared at his hat and brushed it with his hands. He could see her getting closer out of the corner of his eye.

Kid Cheyenne could not understand it but his heart was pounding like a war drum inside his chest. When she was barely five feet from his left shoulder, he tilted his head and looked at her.

He placed the hat over his thick head of hair as she slowly stopped. She was roughly his age by the look of her and had a simple beauty that the Kid liked.

'My name's Olivia,' she said softly.

The Kid had seen many females over the years as he had journeyed from town to town. Fine fancy females dressed in the finest clothes and scores of bargirls who frequented the numerous saloons and cantinas he had visited.

But this female was different.

Olivia wore no face paint and her hair had obviously suffered after a long day of cooking food over a hot stove. Yet she had awakened something in the man who made his living by dishing out death. He could not explain, even to himself, what he was feeling.

He felt like a youngster who had suddenly discovered the existence of the opposite sex. The Kid sighed and adjusted his gun-belt as she stepped even closer.

'Where you going, Kid?' she asked.

Kid Cheyenne felt his sap rising and ran a hand over his reddening features. He swallowed hard and turned to face her square on.

'I ain't too sure, Olivia,' he freely admitted as his mind tried to understand what was happening to him. Whatever it was, it had never happened before. 'I was figuring on finding a hotel and hiring myself a room. I'm tuckered after a long ride from Waco.'

She smiled. 'You don't look like the sort of man who ever gets tired.'

Kid Cheyenne grinned and started to nod as he looked down upon her petite form. For some unexplainable reason he was no longer as weary as he knew he should be.

'You sure have got a way of waking up a man, Olivia,' he said as he inhaled her natural perfume and savoured it. 'I ain't even saddle sore any more.'

Her hand rose up and her fingers gently touched his unshaven face. The Kid felt a strange ripple of excitement tear through his lean body as she continued to awaken something deep inside his soul. Something that had never been awakened before. He looked down upon her longingly. She looked so fresh to the deadly killer and unlike any other woman he had encountered previously.

'I've never met anyone quite like you before, Kid,' she informed. 'I've never said this before to anyone but why don't you stay here with me?'

He cleared his throat as he looked into her eyes. It was an unexpected invitation that he would have willingly sold his soul for.

The Kid stammered. 'Don't sell yourself short for me, Olivia. I ain't worth it.'

'Don't talk yourself down, Kid,' Olivia did not understand her own mixed emotions but there was no way that she thought that she was being used. For the first time in her entire life she had encountered someone that had kindled her eternal flame.

Beads of nervous sweat trickled down the Kid's face and dripped on to her. They had nothing to do with the temperature inside the café.

'I ain't the kinda guy decent womenfolk should tangle with, Olivia,' the Kid admitted as she continued to brush his cheek with her fingers. 'I'm bad news.'

She smiled. It was the sweetest and purest smile he

had ever seen and it clawed at his innards.

'I've never invited a man to stay with me before, Kid,' she announced softly and honestly. 'I'm an old maid and I know it. Nearly thirty and, like the old song says, I ain't ever been kissed.'

He chuckled and ran his fingers through his hair.

'I kinda doubt that anyone as pretty as you ain't never been kissed, darling,' he said.

'Not in over ten or more years, I ain't,' Olivia sighed heavily.

The Kid watched her. He could see the regret and sorrow in her eyes as she remembered things that she had tried to forget for more than a decade.

Olivia silently brushed passed the Kid. He felt an excitement surge through his every fibre as he watched her move to the café door and slide its bolt. She then reached up, pulled down the blind and hooked it on to a nail just below its glass.

Kid Cheyenne could feel his heart pounding even harder as she moved to the window and reached up. She pulled its blind down until none of the street lights could penetrate the café and then secured it. Olivia turned to face him and smiled.

'I live upstairs, Kid,' she said.

The Kid exhaled and lowered his head as his eyes studied her curvaceous body. He watched as she seductively approached him between the tables again.

She paused for a few moments and added.

'I'm going upstairs, Kid,' Olivia said as she walked around the confused gunman and navigated a route between the tables and chairs toward a flight of stairs.

As she reached the bottom of the step she looked over her shoulder and winked at him as she coyly removed her blouse and hung it over her shoulder. 'Follow me if you want to.'

Kid Cheyenne had no idea how he had gotten into this situation but was thankful that he had decided to fill his belly with food instead of rotgut whiskey.

'I surely want to, Olivia,' the Kid heard himself say.

She had no sooner started up the stairs at the rear of the café to her private quarters than the Kid did as she had instructed and started to trail her.

He was like a hound on the trail of a coon. If he had had a tail, he would have wagged it. He wiped his mouth on his bandanna tails and started to smile to himself.

For the first time in his entire adult existence the normally cold-hearted Kid Cheyenne was doing something that was both unplanned and totally unexpected.

As he reached the foot of the stairs, the Kid looked upward and saw the shadow of the shapely Olivia reflected alluringly on the wall. A shiver traced up his spine as he somehow managed to control himself and not howl like a rampant wolf.

He cupped a hand over the glass funnel of a lamp resting on a shelf and blew out its flame. He turned and placed a boot on the bottom step.

The Kid slowly ascended the staircase toward the tempting shadow on the wall. With every step he felt his heart beating faster and faster.

This had nothing to do with why Kid Cheyenne was

in Bloodstone yet he simply did not give a damn. Olivia had found a chink in his armour and the Kid was curious to discover what actually lay inside his normally impregnable façade.

Ever since the ruckus back in Waco he had started to question everything that he had become since the end of the war, when he had discovered that his ability with his guns were a valuable asset. Yet the gunfight in Waco had changed the man known only as Kid Cheyenne. His normally cold-hearted attitude to slaughtering the unwary began to gnaw at his conscience. The further he had ridden into the desert on his way to Bloodstone, the more he had begun to wonder about all the men he had killed over the years.

Who had they been?

Why had men paid for them to be destroyed?

None of the questions sat well with the thoughtful Kid. Maybe he had actually killed the wrong men. Taken the side of those who paid him without ever considering the cost of his quicksilver way with his .45s.

The thoughts troubled the Kid. Since his arrival in the remote settlement the hardened killer had started to wonder who exactly Ben Black actually was and what his motives were for hiring him.

He reached the landing and paused for a few moments as his eyes adjusted to the light of a solitary candle burning in the small but neat bedroom. This was no heavily scented boudoir with a painted female of dubious age waiting for yet another paying suitor.

This was the simple bedroom of an ordinary female

who was willing to risk everything she possessed for one last chance at finding affection in the arms of a stranger.

Kid Cheyenne glanced through the flickering candlelight at the woman he only knew as Olivia. She appeared so vulnerable to his well-travelled eyes. Olivia West wanted to seduce him and yet felt embarrassed by her instinctive actions. Her carnal desires were in total conflict with a lifetime of modesty. He rested a hand on the wall and smiled at her.

She ran into his arms and was welcomed.

SEVENTEEN

The Spinning Wheel saloon had calmed down over the previous couple of hours and the crowd was getting noticeably thinner as gradually the customers disappeared into the streets. Casey O'Hara and his companion had managed to drink half the contents of their whiskey bottle as men moved away from the bar counter as the wall clock started to chime. Every eye automatically glanced at the wall above the door as the tobacco-stained timepiece rang out.

'Midnight already?' Toke York asked as the chimes awoke him from a deep sleep. He yawned, stared at O'Hara and sighed heavily. 'Reckon we'd best head on back to the range, Casey.'

The equally weary O'Hara was about to nod in agreement when he saw the six men rising to their feet beyond the horseshoe-shaped bar counter. He grabbed the skinny arm of his companion and stopped York from getting to his feet.

'Keep rooted, Toke.'

York looked mystified and raised his bushy eye-brows.

'What in tarnation you doing, sonny?' he complained before pulling his arm free of O'Hara's grip. 'It's time for us to high-tail it back to our ranches.'

O'Hara did not say a word for a few moments as he watched Ben Black and his heavily armed men start to move toward the saloon swing doors. Then he grabbed York's head and practically pulled it across the table toward him.

'That's Black and his bunch, Toke,' he whispered without looking away from the liquored-up gunmen. 'They must have bin in here all the time we've bin drinking.'

York slowly turned his head and watched as Black led his gunmen through the handful of remaining customers toward the saloon doors as they rocked on their hinges.

'Look at their guns, Casey,' he stammered. 'Them varmints ain't no cowboys, just like I said. They wouldn't know one end of a steer from the other.'

Casey O'Hara was shaking as he looked across the smoke-filled room as Black and his cohorts pushed their way out into the night air. As the last of the half dozen men left the saloon, O'Hara began to breathe again.

'For a minute there I thought they'd seen us, Toke,' he said as he watched the doors rocking back and forth on their hinges. 'Phew, I ain't ever bin as scared as that in my whole life. For a few moments there I thought they'd start fanning their hammers and finish us off.'

The ranchers waited for what felt like an eternity until the sound of horses riding away from the Spinning Wheel echoed inside the saloon. Both York and O'Hara gave a sigh of relief.

York got to his feet and gave a slight wink at O'Hara as he nervously stood up. They mopped their glistening brows with the tails of their bandannas.

'That was too damn close,' O'Hara said.

'I wasn't scared,' he bluffed. 'I'm too damn drunk to be scared, Casey.'

Both ranchers laughed and made their way toward the swing doors. O'Hara raised a hand to the remaining few patrons inside the heart of the saloon as they pushed their way out on to the boardwalk.

The night air in Bloodstone was still hotter than most places reach during the hours of daylight but the seasoned ranchers were used to it. What they were not used to was being scared of shadows. It did not sit well with either of them.

They paused for a moment on the boardwalk and looked across the street to where their horses were still tethered outside the hardware store. Neither rancher could hear the sound of the departing horses' hoofs any longer. A sense of relief washed their nerves clean as they both stepped down on to the moonlit sand and started to cross toward the horses.

'I'll be glad to get home tonight, Toke,' O'Hara admitted as they neared the narrow waterway in the middle of the street. 'My nerves ain't what they used to be.'

Suddenly an ear-splitting sound filled the night air.

It was like a crazed hornet hurtling toward them. It stopped both ranchers in their tracks. Then, far too late, they realized what it was.

It was a bullet.

O'Hara rocked as the volatile bullet hit him.

Toke York swung on his heels as his friend was knocked off his feet by the brutal impact. Droplets of blood sprayed in the eerie moonlight and a cloud of dust rose up in the lantern light as O'Hara landed on his back beside his friend.

For a few brief moments York was showered by scarlet rain as the sickening gore landed on him and his stricken friend.

'Casey?' York gasped out loud as he stared through the twilight. He dropped on to one knee and studied his friend lying on the sand.

Yet there was no response from O'Hara. A trail of smoke drifted up from his body where the bullet had skewered a path into his body. The burning aroma filled York's nostrils as he hovered over his pal.

It was the unmistakable scent of death.

A pool of blood spread out around the lifeless body of the rancher as he lay totally still on the sand. York shook his prostrate friend a couple of times but there was no sign of life.

Sadness suddenly turned into rage.

York turned his head and squinted down the long street. Then he saw them. The black silhouettes of the six horsemen sent a chill through the rancher as he got back to his feet. York noticed smoke trailing from the barrel of one of the rider's rifles.

Every fibre of the veteran rancher's being knew that they were the Lazy B boys but he could not swear on the Good Book and positively identify them. His clenched fists shook in anger at the line of lethal horsemen, who sat with the light of the moon on their collective backs. York was about to yell out at them to kill him as well when they turned their mounts and thundered away.

Toke York was shaking as the last of the saloon customers and its bartenders rushed out of the Spinning Wheel and gathered around him. The bartenders were the only sober men amongst the small bunch and they checked the body.

None of the gathering had ever witnessed anything as horrific as the sight before them and were all as visibly shaken as York.

One of the bartenders named Charlie Bart moved to the side of the stunned rancher and placed a comforting hand on his shoulder.

'Casey's stone-cold dead, Toke,' the bartender said. 'He got himself a bullet hole in his chest you could ride a chuck wagon through.'

York nodded. 'I know, son. I know.'

'Did you see who done it?'

York bit his lip and looked at the bartender. For a few fleeting heartbeats he considered the question and then shook his head.

'They were too far away,' he sadly noted. 'But I know who done it in my guts. It was either Ben Black or one of his hired scum.'

To the surprise of the men standing in the growing

pool of blood, there was the sound of a door opening and then being closed along the street.

The sound of footsteps in the shadows beneath the porch overhangs echoed around the otherwise quiet street as someone approached the small group. Each man looked at the boardwalk and watched as a man appeared out of the shadows and stepped down on the sand. The tin star on his chest gleamed as the lantern light caught it and its nervous owner.

Three years earlier Harvey Green had found the ideal job for a man who wanted an easy life and a regular pay check. For the skittish man had never liked trouble and, for most of his time as sheriff, Bloodstone had been a peaceful place. When the trouble had started, Green had never truly attempted to discover the culprits behind the random killings.

Green did not like to court danger or trouble.

He had found out a long time before that it did not pay to confront men who were heavily armed and seemed to know how to handle their weaponry.

Sheriff Harvey Green was a man who wanted to live long enough to draw his pension and was determined to achieve that goal.

Green twitched as he stared down at the gruesome sight at his feet. He leaned over and studied the body before returning to his full height and shrugging.

'Reckon he's dead, boys,' the sheriff sighed and looked at the men staring in his direction. 'Nothing I can do here.'

York stared straight at Green. 'Get a posse and hunt them varmints down, Sheriff. The trail is still fresh.'

Sheriff Green shook his head. 'I ain't wasting my time trying to get enough men together to form a posse, Toke. Everybody in Bloodstone is usually drunk at this time of night.'

York sighed heavily. 'I figured as much.'

'Anybody see who gunned down Casey?' the lawman asked drily as he walked around the corpse. 'Any positive sightings of the varmint that did this?'

The bartender closest to O'Hara's body glanced at the sheriff and raised a hand in order to draw the reluctant lawman's attention.

'You got anything to say?' the star packer asked.

'Toke here said he saw a bunch of horsemen at the far end of the street,' the bartender informed the disinterested sheriff.

'Is that so, Toke?' the lawman asked York.

York nodded. 'I sure did.'

'Can you identify them, Toke?' the sheriff stared into the rancher's face and raised his eyebrows. 'Can you be certain who they were?'

Toke York snorted through his nostrils and replied reluctantly. 'Nope, I can't be certain but it had to be Ben Black or one of his gunmen.'

'But you ain't positive,' the lawman grinned and turned his back on the small group before pacing back to his office.

York stared at the sheriff.

'I can't be sure but . . .' the sentence was not allowed to be completed as Green started to shake his head.

'I can't go and arrest Ben Black just coz you got a

gut feeling it might have bin him or one of his boys that killed Casey,' Green announced before turning to the drunken men still standing in the pool of gore. 'Ain't nothing I can do. Haul Casey off to the undertakers and then go home. I'm headed back to my office.'

York kicked at the sand at his feet.

'For god's sake, it had to be Black and his bunch,' he yelled at the back of the departing lawman. The sheriff did not turn back to face the bemused men. He kept on walking back to his office.

The sound of the sheriff's office door being closed behind him as Green entered echoed around the otherwise silent main street.

'He ain't gonna do nothing, Charlie,' York gasped.

'Did you expect anything else from that critter, Toke?' Bart replied sadly. 'He'll be bedded down with a bottle of whiskey before old Casey is even cold.'

'What the hell is going on in Bloodstone, Charlie?' York mumbled.

With a comforting arm around York's shoulder, Charlie Bart pulled the rancher back towards the Spinning Wheel.

'Come on, Toke,' Bart said. 'I'll help you finish that bottle of rye you and Casey left on the card table.'

As the rest of the men carefully lifted O'Hara's body off the sand and started to carry it toward the funeral parlour, Charlie Bart steered the shocked York back into the saloon.

EIGHTEEN

The sound of the shot was still ringing in the ears of the lean observer as he stood beside the open bedroom window and stared down at the amber-illuminated scene. Kid Cheyenne had heard every word through the open window and, just like the enraged York, was certain that Black was the culprit. He gave the sleeping Olivia a quick glance and sighed as he picked up his trail-weary pants.

He did not say a word as he dressed quickly. Yet, even though he was as quiet as he could be, she stirred and awoke.

Olivia rose from the bedsheets and stared through the flickering candlelight at the Kid. She tilted her head and her mane of thick black hair tumbled over her alluring features.

'Where are you going?' she asked quietly.

The Kid smiled at her as he pulled his boots on while leaning against the bedroom wall. Her dreams had been filled with so many joyous colours and as she watched the lean figure tuck in his shirt tails she realized that he had brought something into her existence that had not been there before. She could see the smile on his face as he snuffed the candle's flame with a finger and thumb.

'Go back to sleep, darling,' he whispered as his hand stroked her face gently. 'I've gotta find out a few things. If I don't it'll haunt me.'

Olivia West got up on to her knees and pulled the sheets up under her chin. She stared at the lean man who had shared her ecstasy for more than an hour. Her heart quickened as she thought of him running out on her.

'Are you leaving because you've had what you wanted, Kid?' her voice trembled as she uttered the words. 'Are you running out on me?'

Kid Cheyenne gave a slight laugh and shook his head at the suggestion. He was suddenly aware of what the handsome female thought and feared.

'You couldn't be more wrong. I figured on coming back,' he declared. 'If that's OK with you, Olivia?'

'That's fine with me, Kid,' she sniffed. 'That's about as fine as can be.'

The Kid nodded.

Her expression changed from sadness to unbridled joy. Tears filled her eyes but his fingers wiped them away as he picked up his black hat and placed it on his head. The Kid lifted his hand-tooled gun-belt and walked slowly to the door and on to the landing. When he reached the top of the stairs, he paused and looked back at her.

111

The Kid could not understand the change she had brought to him but he was thankful. During the war he had turned into a killing machine and made a small fortune from his uncanny abilities since the conflict ended but until now the Kid had never felt truly alive. He had wandered from one killing job to the next and did others' bidding without thought or question.

The sweet female had somehow managed to change him without even trying. He had found the one thing that he had been looking for without even trying. He stared at her and suddenly realized that his life until now had been nothing more than mere existence. Her sweet charms had done something none of his opponents' bullets had ever been able to do. She had rekindled his heart.

'Get some sleep,' he said softly. 'I'll be back when I've satisfied my curiosity.'

'Promise?'

'Yep,' he drawled. 'I promise.'

Defying his desire to go straight back to her and continue his pleasuring, Kid Cheyenne walked down the steps towards the dark café. With each step he buckled his gun-belt around his hips and then tied the long leather laces that hung from his holsters around his thighs.

As the Kid negotiated a route between the café tables toward the front door, he knew that only death could stop him from returning to her.

Olivia lay back on the bed and then grabbed the soft feather-filled pillow that still held his fragrance.

She pulled it to her naked body, inhaled it and then closed her eyes.

'He'll be back,' she sighed confidently. 'He'll be back.'

NINETEEN

There were just two people in the Spinning Wheel sat sharing a bottle of whiskey at one of its tables. One of the bartenders had gone home while his fellow server of hard liquor rested on his elbows and stared into the shocked face of Toke York as the rancher repeatedly mulled over the horrifying events of only fifteen minutes earlier.

'I can't understand it, Charlie,' York said for the umpteenth time as he downed another glass of the powerful whiskey. 'Casey tried to warn me that it was foolhardy coming in here. We'd both seen Black and his boys come in here but I was too damn cocky and insisted we have us a drink.'

Charlie Bart poured himself another drink and swallowed it as York kept on talking. He knew that the two ranchers had been close and could understand why the veteran York was so distraught.

'Me and Casey thought that Black hadn't noticed us,' York sighed as he shook his head and frowned. 'Him and his boys never even looked in our direction as they moseyed out on to the street but they must have spotted us.'

'Take it easy, Toke,' Charlie refilled their glasses. 'You're beating yourself up for no reason.'

York squinted across the table. 'We even heard the varmints ride away from the saloon. Casey thought it was safe for us to leave.'

'I watched Black and his boys leave,' Bart said. 'You're right, they never even looked to where you and Casey were sitting.'

Suddenly both men's attention was drawn to the swing doors as the sound of heavy boots could be heard coming along the boardwalk outside the saloon. They stared at the doors as a hand was placed on the top of one of them.

'Who in tarnation is that?' York stammered.

Before the bartender could reply, the door was pushed inward and the tall figure entered. Kid Cheyenne glanced around the empty saloon and then focused on the two seated men close to the counter. He touched his hat brim as he strode towards the seated men.

Kid Cheyenne paused a few feet from the table and looked at both men in turn. He then dragged an empty chair away from the green baize and sat down between them.

'Howdy,' the Kid said in a low whisper. 'They call me the Kid. I'm sorry to interrupt but the shooting a few minutes back made me kinda curious.'

'This ain't a good time, stranger,' the bartender said as he studied the seated man with the grips of his holstered weapons strapped to his hips. 'Toke York here just lost his best friend. He'd a mite upset.'

The Kid looked at the tortured expression on York's face, then pulled out a long slim cigar and bit off its end. He spat at the unswept floor.

'Did you happen to see who killed your friend, Toke?' he asked as he scratched a match with his thumbnail and slowly raised its flame to the tip of the cigar. He puffed a few times and then flicked the blackened ember at the floor.

York's expression changed. He leaned forward, stared at the Kid and blinked hard to clear his vision.

'How come you're interested?' he asked. 'I ain't never seen you in these parts before. What do you want here?'

Kid Cheyenne inhaled deeply and then slowly blew smoke at the floor. He then looked up into the watery eyes of the rancher and shrugged.

'I'll ask you again,' he drawled. 'Did you see who killed your friend?'

Toke York sat back on his chair and downed the glass of whiskey in his hand. As the fiery fumes burned a path down into his guts, he studied the lean stranger more carefully.

'I can't tell a lie and say I seen Ben Black pull the trigger that killed my pal but it was him OK,' York rambled. 'Him and his boys were at the far end of the street sitting on their nags and one of them was holding a smoking rifle in the air. Black had just left the saloon and ridden away. It had to be him.'

Thoughtfully, Kid Cheyenne nodded and pulled

the cigar from his lips. He rubbed his jawline with this knuckles and then leaned forward and rested his elbows on the green surface of the card table.

'Seems to me that this Ben Black character and his hired help have got themselves an agenda,' the Kid said. 'I'm told that there are three cattle spreads in Bloodstone. Seems to me that Black and his boys want to reduce that to just one.'

Both York and Bart looked blankly at the stranger. Neither man knew what he meant. It was the rancher who piped up first to hopefully get an explanation that they could understand.

'What do you mean?' York enquired as he refilled his and the bartender's glasses with the last of the whiskey and lifted it to hip lips. 'What in tarnation is a darn agenda?'

'Black's got a plan,' the Kid said.

'You're damn right, Kid,' York agreed. 'Once I'm dead, he'll have no competition in these parts.'

Kid Cheyenne took a long pull on his cigar. He allowed the strong smoke to dwell for a while in his lungs before blowing it at the sawdust beneath the table.

'I'd never heard of Ben Black before yesterday,' he started to explain. 'I got a wire from the galoot for me to come here to Bloodstone. Now I'm hearing a lot of bad things about this Black character and it don't sit right with me.'

The weary bartender looked at the Kid.

'Why'd he send for you?' he asked.

'I'm what folks call a gunslinger,' the Kid replied

dryly as he took another long pull on his cigar. 'I get hired to kill folks for other folks.'

Both the rancher and Bart were shocked by the Kid's honesty and yet they suddenly sensed danger. Even their drunken eyes could tell that the man seated between them was exactly what he had admitted to be. They looked at his gun grips protruding from the hand-tooled holsters and both men swallowed hard.

'Did you just say that you're a hired gunman, sonny?' York stuttered and then drained the whiskey from his glass. He looked at Bart but the bartender just sat there open-mouthed. York then returned his attention to their uninvited guest. 'Black sent for you and you obliged the bastard by coming here?'

Kid Cheyenne tapped the ash from his cigar and then placed it in the corner of his mouth. His narrowed eyes flashed between the startled pair before settling on the rancher.

'You could say that,' the Kid began before adding. 'But in the last few hours I've learned a lot about this Black critter and I don't like what I've learned.'

York pushed the empty bottle at the bartender. 'Get us a fresh bottle, Charlie. I seem to have sobered up since this hombre joined us.'

Bart got to his feet and walked around the horseshoe-shaped bar counter. Within a few heartbeats he returned with a bottle of amber liquor in one hand and a fresh glass in the other. He placed both on the table and then wiped the sweat from his face with his shirt sleeve.

'You hire yourself out to do other critters' killing?' York slurred as he watched Bart pull the cork from the bottle neck with his teeth and fill all three glasses. 'Is that what you're telling us, Kid?'

Kid Cheyenne gave a nod of his head.

'You mean you'll kill anybody if some varmint pays you to do so?' the bartender managed to say before his shaking hand lifted his glass and he threw its contents into his mouth.

The Kid nodded again.

Toke York's eyes widened as he suddenly felt very vulnerable sitting so close to the well-armed stranger. He pushed the third glass of hard liquor toward the Kid.

'Who did Black want you to kill?' he managed to ask.

Kid Cheyenne lifted the glass and took a sip of the powerful liquor before locking eyes on the aged rancher. He licked his lips and then placed the glass back down on the baize.

'By what I've learned since arriving in Bloodstone,' the Kid stated confidently as he stared at York. 'It seems that Ben Black is mighty ambitious. I can think of only two men he'd truly like killed and one of them is already in the funeral parlour.'

'Casey,' York sighed sadly.

'By my reckoning, that leaves just you,' Kid Cheyenne said as he toyed with his cigar and watched his companions.

Toke York felt his heart pounding inside his shirt. The stranger had not taken his eyes off the rancher in

119

more than five minutes and it was like being studied by a mountain cat.

'You didn't shoot old Casey, did you son?' he asked.

The Kid raised an eyebrow and shook his head.

'Nope, I was busy when that shot was fired,' he revealed.

'But Black sent for you,' York repeated. 'You said that folks hire you to do their killing for them. Did he send for you to kill me and Casey?'

Kid Cheyenne shrugged.

'I don't know the answer to that one, old timer,' he said. 'But even if that was his intention it don't mean that I'd agree to do his killing.'

Both the bartender and the rancher were utterly bemused.

'But you said that you're a hired killer,' the bartender piped up as he held on to his empty glass with both shaking hands. 'I don't savvy this.'

Kid Cheyenne rose to his feet and looked down at the seated pair before him. He dropped his cigar into a spittoon and started to nod thoughtfully.

'I've done my share of killing over the years,' he explained as he gripped the chair and slid it under the card table. 'But a man grows tired of it. Every single man I've killed seems to have kinfolk crawling out of the woodwork. They want revenge and over the last couple of days I've had to kill folks simply because they're trying to kill me.'

York got unsteadily to his feet and looked up into the lean features of the tall stranger. He placed a hand on the Kid's arm and drew his full attention.

'You ain't gonna do Black's dirty work for him, are you?' he asked.

'I surely doubt it.' Kid Cheyenne pulled away and started to walk through the sawdust back to the swing doors. He rested a hand on the top of the doors and glanced back at the feeble old rancher.

Toke York did not know why, but he trusted the lean gunman.

The Kid stared at the two saddle horses outside the hardware store thoughtfully. He looked down at York.

'I ain't even met Ben Black but I don't like the critter one bit, friend,' he declared. 'He seems to want all his rivals six feet under and that ain't sociable.'

'What you figuring on doing, Kid?' York heard himself ask the tall stranger. 'Don't head on out to the Lazy B to meet Black. It ain't safe for anyone to ride out on the range after sundown. Me and Casey have had too many of our cowhands shot out there.'

The Kid pushed the doors out toward the street. He paused momentarily and then looked back at the concerned rancher.

'Can I borrow one of them horses over by the hardware store?' he asked York. 'My own quarter horse is in the livery stable resting up.'

Toke York rushed to the side of the lethal gunman.

'You can't go out there, Kid,' he pressed. 'There are six of them and they're all sporting shooting rigs as fine as that one you got strapped around your belly. It'd be suicide.'

The Kid shook his head.

'Why would they shoot at me?' he grinned. 'Black

121

sent for me and I'm just paying him a call.'

'Him and his boys like killing anyone from either the Twisted Bar or Double C, sonny,' he declared. 'They also know I'm still in Bloodstone and might intend on picking me off when I ride home.'

Kid Cheyenne walked out on to the boardwalk and stared at the pair of horses opposite. He looked back at the rancher thoughtfully.

'Which is your horse?' he asked.

'The grey gelding,' York answered. 'Why?'

'I'm borrowing it,' the Kid explained.

Kid Cheyenne stepped down on to the sandy street and strolled toward the two tethered mounts. His mind was full of contradictions of why he was here in this remote settlement and he did not like it. As he reached the pair of mounts at the hitching rail he patted the grey on its rump and then grabbed its securely tied reins. The Kid pulled the long leathers free and slowly led the gelding away from the other mount until its nose was aimed at the lake and the range beyond its sparkling water.

For the first time in his bloody career as a hired gunman, Kid Cheyenne was not simply going to collect his fee and do his paymaster's bidding. Since the war he had become little more than a cold-hearted mercenary and never questioned the reasons behind his being hired to taunt the unwary into a gunfight.

Now he felt differently.

The last few days had seen him use his brutal abilities in order to defend himself. He had lost count of the men he had killed but it had sickened him.

There was no profit in killing folks with revenge burning in their hearts. It was a total waste of ammunition.

The Kid glanced across the wide street and up at the window above the small café. For a fleeting moment he thought that he had caught sight of the trusting Olivia behind the lace drapes watching him. Then a gentle breeze moved the drape and he realized that there was no one there.

Kid Cheyenne touched his hat brim to the window, rested a hand on the saddle-horn, stepped into its stirrup and gracefully mounted the grey gelding. He steadied the horse and noticed that the old rancher was still watching him.

He repeated the action of touching the Stetson's brim and Toke York returned the salute.

The horse started to trot as the Kid tapped his boots against its flanks. From his high perch atop the grey, Kid Cheyenne could see the lights of the three ranch houses reflected in the lake as he rode steadily toward the moonlit range.

'This ain't smart, Kid,' he whispered to himself as the grey gathered pace. 'It's probably the dumbest damn thing you've ever done.'

TWENTY

The gelded grey started to round the lake as the Kid studied the fertile range that led to the otherwise perilous desert. He held his reins to his chest and stopped the mount from returning to the Twisted Bar ranch. Kid Cheyenne had another destination for Toke York's horse and that lay a few miles from the damp ground that fringed the sparkling lake. The Kid leaned back on his saddle until its cantle pressed into the base of his spine and stared at the moon.

He then returned his narrowed eyes to what lay before him.

He had never seen so many steers before. The moonlight seemed to reflect off the long horns as they milled around the well-nourished ground before him.

The lights of the Lazy B ranch house were bright in the otherwise eerie landscape and made a good target for the horseman to aim the grey toward.

The Kid had no idea what he was going to do when

124

he finally reached the distant lantern light but every fibre of his being told him that this was one fight for which he was ill-equipped.

Never in all his days had he ever willingly ridden into the unknown the way he was doing now. He tapped his spurs and got the grey moving faster. Kid Cheyenne knew only too well that men such as Ben Black surrounded themselves with gunmen for only one reason. They were paid to take the first bullets in a fight and allow their boss to pick off their foes.

The gelding was moving faster beneath the lean horseman as he guided the horse between the hundreds of grazing long horn steers. The steers did not like being disturbed and bellowed at the heavens as the rider continued on.

He had no idea how many men Black actually had to hide behind but he knew that he had five cohorts when he had left town. That might be all of them, the Kid thought. He hoped it was anyway.

As mud splattered up from his mount's hoofs, the Kid caught a brief glimpse of two horsemen to his left.

The Kid drew rein and stopped the snorting animal.

He rose up and balanced in his stirrups as he squinted across the distance between himself and the two other riders. Whoever they were, he mused, they were not from the Lazy B. They were too far away and much closer to the Double C spread and its neighbour the Twisted Bar.

Kid Cheyenne was not a man known for his curiosity but he wondered who they were. He swung the grey hard around and used the tails of his long leathers to whip the gelding's tail.

The horse had probably never been ridden so hard before but was well up to the task and thundered across the range towards both the horsemen.

The closer the Kid got to the two riders, the clearer they became to his tormented eyes as they worked hard to see in the strange moonlit area.

It was obvious to Kid Cheyenne that they were not hired gunmen for neither reacted the way gunmen always do when faced by a rider heading straight at them.

They had to be cowboys, the Kid reasoned.

Real cowboys, unlike the men in Ben Black's employ.

Kid Cheyenne started to draw back on his reins as he neared the pair of bemused cowpokes. As the grey gelding's hoofs skidded to a halt beneath him, the Kid continued to watch their faces carefully.

They appeared like startled jack rabbits.

Both cowboys sat and watched as the Kid stopped his mount a few feet away from them. Neither had moved a muscle during the entire time they had been observing him.

'What spread do you boys work for?' Kid Cheyenne asked as his horse bowed its head and snorted.

The cowboys looked at one another and then at the lean rider before them. The closest pushed his ten-gallon hat back until it hung by its drawstring against the crown of his head.

'Me and Seth here are Double C cowpokes,

stranger,' he replied before leaning over his horse's mane and studying the Kid carefully. 'Who might you be?'

'They call me Kid,' the infamous hired gunslinger replied as he steadied the grey. 'I've got some sad news for you boys.'

Both cowpunchers sat silently and waited for the sad news.

'A couple of hours back your boss got himself shot,' the Kid said. 'He's dead.'

'Casey's dead?' one of the cowboys repeated.

Kid Cheyenne nodded. 'Somebody shot him and then high-tailed it back here on to the range. Did either of you see six riders earlier?'

They nodded in unison.

'We seen the Lazy B bunch returning from Bloodstone,' one of them informed. 'They were riding fast and headed over to the ranch house yonder.'

The Kid rubbed his jaw thoughtfully. He turned the grey gelding and stared out across the vast range at the Twisted Bar. He glanced over his shoulder at the pair of cowboys.

'Round up the rest of the boys from the Twisted Bar and Double C spreads,' the Kid ordered. 'Will you do that for me?'

'What for, stranger?' the other cowpuncher asked.

'Head on into Bloodstone,' Kid Cheyenne added as he gathered up his loose leathers in his hands. 'Toke York is in the Spinning Wheel drinking. He's really shook up about Casey getting killed and I figure he needs protecting.'

Both men nodded.

The Kid swung the gelding around and then spurred.

TWENTY-ONE

Ben Black still held the Winchester repeating rifle that he had used a half hour earlier to kill Casey O'Hara before leading his five gunmen back to the Lazy B. He crossed the large room and sat down on his padded chair before the fireplace. Black was grinning from ear to ear as his men helped themselves to more drinks and rested before the fire's flames.

Then Black's mood suddenly changed as he glared at Hank Smith. The gunman felt nervous as he watched Black push the rifle's hand guard down to expel a bullet casing. Smith lowered his whiskey from his mouth as Black jerked the lever back up sternly.

'You said Kid Cheyenne was in Bloodstone, Hank,' Black said before levelling the barrel of the Winchester at his henchman. 'How come we didn't find the critter?'

Smith was shaking as most men do when staring down the business end of a primed rifle. His eyes darted to the faces of his four fellow gunmen as though looking for support. None of the men seemed interested and just continued drinking.

'He's in Bloodstone, Ben,' Smith insisted. 'The blacksmith told you that. I weren't imagining it. I seen the varmint.'

Black stared along the barrel of the rifle as he kept it aimed at Smith. He then smiled again and lowered the deadly weapon as he recalled his latest victim.

'When Billy spotted them ranchers in the Spinning Wheel and told me, I knew that we'd be able to pick one of them off,' the owner of the Lazy B chuckled. 'It was so easy. I could have killed the both of them as they started crossing the street.'

Cody Carson filled his glass with whiskey again and then turned to look at his boss. 'How come you didn't?'

Black placed the rifle against the wall and rose up. He walked to the table where the drinks awaited.

'Good question, Cody,' Black retorted. 'I had intended getting Kid Cheyenne to kill both of them. That's why I wired for him to come here but sometimes things take a different course.'

Carson downed his whiskey and watched as the rancher filled an empty glass to the brim. He knew that Black was far more dangerous than any of them.

'Do you reckon this Kid Cheyenne critter is worth his fee, Ben?' he asked as he watched Black inhaling the fumes from his liquor. 'We could wipe out every damn cowboy on the range without the help of some fancy gunslinger.'

Black went thoughtful as he stared at the inviting glass of whiskey a few inches from his awaiting mouth.

His eyes flashed at Carson.

'Yeah, you might be right, Cody,' he mumbled before filled his mouth with the powerful liquor and then swallowing. 'I reckon we don't really need the help of this gunslinger. I shouldn't have telegraphed him.'

'What you gonna do when he finally shows up here, Ben?' Carson moved closer to the dubious rancher. 'I've heard that he ain't the type to take kindly to being fired from a job after he's come so far.'

The face of Ben Black looked anxious as he considered the problem. He refilled his glass and looked at his gunmen scattered around the room. He had heard that Kid Cheyenne was faster with his guns than anyone in his particular trade. None of his men would stand a chance against the Kid.

'It might be cheaper if we just let the Kid kill Toke York like I originally planned,' he muttered thoughtfully.

'But how much is that gonna cost, Ben?' Carson whispered in his boss's ear. 'I've heard that Kid Cheyenne asks $10,000 to kill anyone.'

Black swung on his heels and stared Cody Carson straight in his unshaven face. His eyebrows frowned at the gunman.

'How much?'

'Ten thousand bucks, Ben,' Carson repeated.

'Are you sure?' Black queried.

Cody Carson simply nodded and then drank his whiskey. He moved to a soft chair and sat down. His and every other set of eyes in the ranch house watched as Black paced around the room.

'I'll call it off,' Black said. 'I ain't paying that kinda money to anyone. I'll tell Kid Cheyenne that I don't need his services and send him back to Waco. Yeah, that's what I'll do. I'll call it off.'

'I've heard he charges the same fee either way, Ben,' Jake Cooper informed. 'He don't cotton to folks that welch on a deal and, in his mind you made a deal by contacting him.'

Black stopped pacing. 'That's plumb ridiculous. How can he charge the same fee even if he don't kill someone?'

'Oh, he'll kill someone, Ben,' Carson told the assembly.

'What?' Black muttered.

'He'll kill you,' Carson sighed. 'They reckon he's got no sense of humour. It's a hard ride here from Waco and in his mind you'll have to pay him or else.'

Ben Black rested his hip on the edge of the drinks table and stared at the sod floor of the ranch house. His men watched as he silently mumbled to himself.

Then Hank Smith turned and stared out of the window at the moonlit land outside the ranch house. For a few moments he simply sipped his drink and then he moved closer to the glass panes.

'Hey, Ben,' he said several times until he drew Black's attention. Black glanced at his hireling standing ashen-faced by the window.

'What, Hank?' the rancher sighed. 'You look like you just seen a ghost.'

Black was correct. Smith looked exactly like

132

someone who had just seen a ghost as he stared at his boss. He was visibly shaken by what he had just witnessed out in the eerie moonlight heading straight at the ranch house.

'He ain't no ghost but he's coming,' Smith stammered. 'The same critter that I seen in the livery is riding straight towards us, Ben.'

Suddenly Smith had Black's full attention. The grim-faced rancher lowered his glass and glared at the terrified gunman as Smith watched the unexpected sight through the window.

'The Kid?' Black checked. 'You're saying that the Kid is heading here?'

'Yep, the Kid.' Smith nodded as the rest of the gunmen gathered around the window and watched the rider steering the gelded grey toward the ranch house. 'He sure is a mighty brave *hombre*.'

Ben Black inspected his guns swiftly and then looked at his assembled henchmen. He shook a fist at the bunch as they gathered up their weapons frantically.

'None of you draw them guns,' he ordered. 'Not unless I tell you to. Savvy?'

'He's on our side, ain't he?' Jake Cooper asked as he slid his .45 back into its holster and watched as Black slowly moved toward the door.

'I ain't taking any chances with Kid Cheyenne, Jake,' the rancher mumbled under his breath.

TWENTY-TWO

Kid Cheyenne could hear the frantic activity inside the ranch house as he approached. He drew rein and stopped the gelded grey beside the half a dozen saddle horses tied to the long twisted hitching pole outside the long structure. Without a moment's hesitation, the lean horseman looped a leg over the head of his mount and slid to the ground.

The haunting moonlight gave the entire area the appearance of a graveyard. The honed instincts of the gunfighter knew that guns could appear from behind any of the structures at any time. His eyes darted around the area in search of any unseen assassins as he toyed with his reins.

Only when he was satisfied that none of Black's fellow gunmen were outside the structure did the Kid push the tails of his top coat over his holstered .45s. He then flicked the leather safety loops off his gun hammers and returned his full attention to the sturdy door before him.

He was well aware of the men who resided inside the building. He knew that none of them could be trusted and he should not even have ridden to the Lazy B. Yet he had come to this place because the mysterious Ben Black had sent for him, and that gnawed at the Kid's innards.

He wondered why Black had required the services of a notorious gunslinger when he was supposedly surrounded by hombres of similar abilities.

It made no sense to the Kid.

Maybe he would discover the truth behind the solid door.

He stepped away from the grey horse and waited. The Kid knew that they had watched his approach and were fully aware of his presence in the courtyard.

Then suddenly a voice yelled out from the safety of the adobe structure and drew the Kid's attention.

'Is that you, Kid?'

A sly smirk etched the Kid's face as the fingers of his left hand pulled a long cigar from his inside pocket, placed it between his teeth and he bit. He spat at the ground. Without ever taking his eyes off the door, be returned the cigar to the corner of his mouth.

'Yep, I'm the critter you've bin expecting,' the Kid called back as he scratched a match with his thumbnail. 'All the way from Waco. Are you Ben Black?'

As the match flame touched the tip of his cigar and the Kid filled his lungs with cigar smoke, he watched the door open up before him. Lamp light spilled out from the house as Black emerged with his gun drawn.

'I'm Black,' the rancher snarled.

'I figured as much,' the Kid said through a cloud of smoke.

'How'd we know that you're Kid Cheyenne?' Black shouted across the distance between them as two of his henchmen flanked him. 'There's bin a lot folks killed out here on the range lately and for all we know you're the varmint that killed them.'

Kid Cheyenne pulled the cigar from his mouth and studied its red hot glowing tip for a few moments before returning it to his mouth. His eyes narrowed as they burned into Black.

'We both know that it was you that done all the killing so far, Black,' the Kid said, before starting to walk straight at the man who was still aiming a gun straight at him. 'By what I've heard, you didn't really need to call on my services.'

Black and his men backed away from the entrance as Kid Cheyenne strode into the ranch house and studied the room and its occupants carefully.

'You can't prove that, Kid,' Black chuckled as he and his men surrounded the tall stranger. 'Nobody can prove that me and the boys are behind any of these killings.'

Kid Cheyenne turned and faced the men, and noted that every one of them had their weaponry holstered. He concentrated on Black and stared with unblinking eyes at the man, who seemed familiar to the hired gunfighter.

'I seem to recall your face, Black,' he said as he rested his hands on his ivory gun grips. 'Have we ever tangled? I've got me a mighty long memory.'

136

Ben Black looked suddenly disturbed by the remark.

'We've never met, Kid,' he insisted.

Kid Cheyenne raised his eyebrows and smiled.

'Maybe you had a different name back then,' he taunted before turning his back on the six gunmen and moving to the table, where whiskey bottles and glasses were assembled. As he started to pour himself a glass of the amber liquor, he looked over his shoulder at Black. 'Who do you want killed, Black?'

The question was unexpected. The Kid had already put the rancher on the back foot by telling him that he remembered him and that troubled Black. Now the Kid had changed the subject and was asking who Black had in mind to be killed.

Ben Black moved closer to the seemingly unconcerned Kid and watched as the lean stranger downed the whiskey. A smile came to his face as he studied the lean figure standing in the centre of his house. He had never seen a more expensive shooting rig strapped around anyone's waist before and he was impressed.

'I'd say you were a man who knows how to handle his guns by the look of them hog-legs, Kid,' Black muttered as he strolled around the gunfighter like a cowpoke inspecting a new saddle horse. 'I figure you must be the hombre I wired.'

Kid Cheyenne drew more cigar smoke into his lungs and turned to face Black and his men. If he had any fear in his body the Kid kept it well concealed.

'Who do you want killed, Black?' he repeated. 'Like

I said, it's a long ride from Waco and I intend getting paid for my saddle sores.'

Black holstered his six-shooter and rubbed his face with both hands. He started to nod to himself as he poured whiskey into a glass.

'I want Toke York of the Twisted Bar killed, Kid,' he eventually admitted. 'I want it done so that no one can point a finger in our direction and say we did it.'

Kid Cheyenne gave a nod of his head.

'That'll be $20,000,' he said. 'Cash money.'

The words stunned Ben Black. It was like being hit by a sledgehammer. The rancher staggered and nearly spilled his whiskey as he absorbed the words.

'How much?' he gasped.

'Twenty thousand bucks, Black,' Kid Cheyenne said again as he moved back toward the door slowly. 'That's my fee. Take it or leave it but either way you'll pay for dragging me out to this damn place.'

Black rushed to the side of the lean Kid and stopped him from walking out into the moonlight. He stared into the emotionless face.

'How can you charge that kinda money just to kill someone, Kid?' he ranted. 'I just picked off Casey O'Hara for the cost of a rifle bullet. Twenty thousand bucks is ridiculous.'

'That's my price, Black,' the Kid snarled as he glared down at the sweating rancher. 'I don't give a damn that you just killed another of your rivals for nothing.'

Black trailed the gunslinger out into the eerie light of the courtyard as the Kid headed back toward his waiting mount. The rancher placed himself between the lean gunman and the hitching rail.

Kid Cheyenne stared through his cigar smoke at Black.

'Get out of the way,' he drawled ominously. 'I'm leaving.'

Black frowned furiously.

'We ain't finished talking yet,' he snarled.

'I have,' the Kid said.

Black stepped closer to the Kid. 'You ain't going no place, Kid Cheyenne. You ain't leaving here.'

Kid Cheyenne tilted his head and spat the cigar into the face of the rancher. Red sparks filled the night air as the cigar bounced off Black's face. Before either the rancher or his hired gunmen could react, the Kid had grabbed Black around the neck, turned him to face his men and dragged the six-shooter from the rancher boss's holster.

The sound of the gun hammer being cocked filled the courtyard as the Kid held Black in check.

'Tell your men to throw their guns out here before I break your damn neck, Black,' the Kid said in the rancher's ear. He loosened his grip just enough for Black to obey.

'Do it,' he croaked as he felt the cold steel of the gun barrel press into his temple. 'Toss your hog-legs out here on the sand.'

Reluctantly the five men threw their .45s out on to the sand at Black's feet. As the last of the six-shooters hit the sand, the Kid released his grip and pushed the startled rancher toward the open doorway.

As Black steadied himself, he turned. Kid Cheyenne had already pulled his reins free of the twisted hitching pole and mounted the grey. The six men stared up at the gun held in the Kid's hand and trained upon them.

'What'll we do, Ben?' Cody Carson asked as the rancher stumbled back into his men.

Kid Cheyenne backed the gelded grey away from the house as he aimed the gun at the men. When he was about twenty feet away from the group he stopped his mount.

'Twenty thousand dollars, Black,' he repeated the large sum of money and grinned. 'That's what you owe me and my saddle sores. I want the money tomorrow in cash.'

Billy Kane started to dash for the pile of guns when the Kid squeezed the trigger of Black's gun. The gunman gave out a scream as he felt the bullet tear through his boot leather and into his shin. Kane crumpled to the sand before his cohorts.

The Kid threw the smoking weapon to his side and turned the grey. Black and his men watched as the Kid spurred the gelding and thundered into the moonlight.

A cloud of hoof dust rose into the night air as the grey sprinted away from the Lazy B and headed for the vast herd of long horn steers grazing on the range around the lake.

'My leg's busted, Ben,' Kane whimpered.

'Shut the hell up, Billy,' Black growled.

'But I'm bleeding,' Kane clutched his boot as blood

140

squirted out of the bullet hole in its leather.

'You ain't dead though,' the rancher snarled and kicked his hireling hard. 'That critter could have killed the whole bunch of us if he'd wanted to. We're all lucky he didn't.'

'Why didn't he kill us if he's that good with his guns?' Kane got to his feet and leaned on Carson. He could feel the blood in his boot as his busted peg bent under his weight.

'He wants the twenty thousand bucks he figures I owe him,' Black replied. 'Kid Cheyenne ain't no fool. If he'd killed me I couldn't pay him.'

Hank Smith moved nervously closer to the rancher. 'Are you gonna pay that varmint, Ben? Seems a darn waste of money if you ask me.'

The rest of the bunch grunted in agreement.

'I'll pay him OK.' Black gritted his teeth as he watched the horseman disappear swiftly into the vast herd of long horn steers grazing near the lake. 'Not with cash but with lead.'

'What we gonna do, Ben?' Carson asked as he propped up the groaning Kane.

There was a devilish look in Black's eyes as he started to nod to his gang. Then the rancher beamed in anticipation of what he had decided to do to the notorious gunfighter.

'I don't know what you're gonna do but I'm gonna kill that bastard,' Black snarled. 'Mark my words, boys. Kid Cheyenne is already dead. He just don't know it yet.'

The men started picking up their guns off the sand.

None of them dared say a word to the seething rancher.

Black swung on his heels and looked at the gathered men who faced him. He snapped his fingers.

'Saddle up six fresh horses,' he told them. 'We're gonna take Billy to the Doc's and then the rest of us are gonna wait for that bastard to show himself.'

'You intending facing the Kid head on, Ben?' Smith stammered as he pushed his .45 in his holster.

Black smirked.

'They reckon that even an elephant don't stand a chance if he gets caught in the crossfire of enough guns, Hank.' The rancher gave out a belly laugh. 'The Kid is about to find out that it don't pay to tangle with Ben Black.'

TWENTY-THREE

Kid Cheyenne had lost count of how many men he had sent to meet their maker without ever suffering a scratch. In the execution business that meant he could demand the highest price for his bloody expertise. People paid whatever price he quoted and knew the danger of not doing so far outweighed the large sums the infamous gunslinger knew his skills were worth.

That was until now.

As he rode back into Bloodstone he knew that he had finally found one man who was seemingly refusing to pay the sum he had demanded.

Kid Cheyenne had plucked out a figure from thin air and told Ben Black that was the amount he wanted. In truth, he knew that the rancher would never pay anywhere close to $20,000, and that suited him just fine.

He did not like Black and knew that the devious rancher would try to kill him before he paid him his chosen fee. He drew rein outside the saloon, dropped from his saddle and looped the reins around the

143

hitching pole. As he stepped up on to the boardwalk he could still see the two men drinking inside the Spinning Wheel where he had left them. He paused for a moment and glanced up the long street. The saloon was the only place with its street lanterns still lit. Bloodstone had gone quiet since he had ridden out to the range, he thought.

As Kid Cheyenne rested a hand on the top of the swing doors, he heard both men call out to him. The Kid turned and then entered the saloon. The smell of stale beer and a multitude of other less fragrant aromas filled his flared nostrils as he marched across the floorboards toward the seated pair.

'How in tarnation did you manage to get back here in one piece, Kid?' York asked as he and Charlie Bart shared a pot of freshly made coffee at the card table.

The Kid sat down and looked at both men in turn.

'What you mean, old-timer?' he asked the veteran cattle rancher. 'I wasn't in any danger.'

Bart shook his head at the calmness of the Kid.

'You must have ice for blood, Kid,' he said before pushing his tin cup toward the infamous gunfighter and filling it with the strong beverage. 'Nobody in Bloodstone would have the guts to ride to the Lazy B after all the folks that have bin gunned down.'

The Kid lifted the steaming cup to his lips and took a mouthful of its strong contents. He lowered it slightly and stared through its steam at the rancher.

'I kinda put a fox in Black's henhouse, Toke,' he admitted.

'What you mean, Kid?' York downed his sobering

144

brew and indicated to the bartender to refill his tin cup. 'What have you done?'

Kid Cheyenne smiled. 'Let's just say that Black and his boys will be coming into town looking for me pretty soon.'

'Why?' Bart wondered as he poured more coffee into York's cup.

'I upset the varmint,' the Kid answered.

Toke York drew back and studied the stranger that until an hour or so earlier he had never met. His expression was confused as he stared at the Kid.

'What in tarnation have you done?' he asked.

The Kid looked between both seated men and then he rested his back against the spindles of his hard chair. He pushed the brim of his hat off his face and took another mouthful of the coffee before placing the empty tin vessel down on the baize.

'I baited a trap,' he smiled. 'I told Black that if he wanted to hire my services it would cost him $20,000.'

York's jaw dropped.

'What kinda service do you provide for that kinda money, sonny?' the rancher asked.

Before Kid Cheyenne could answer, the distinctive sound of horses' hoofs filled the saloon. York looked in horror at the bartender and then at the hired gunman, who quickly rose to his feet and pushed his coat tails over his gun grips.

'That sounds like a bunch of riders, sonny,' the rancher said shakily. 'Black and his boys are here already.'

Kid Cheyenne did not say a word.

145

He turned on his heels and strode purposefully towards the swing doors. The lean gunfighter looked out into the darkness as York and Bart sat shaking in their boots.

As the Kid stared into the eerie moonlight of the otherwise dark street he caught a glimpse of the approaching riders. He looked at his terrified companions.

'It ain't Black and his gunmen,' he drawled.

Slightly bewildered, Toke York got to his feet and stared at the lean gunfighter. His watery eyes watched as the Kid rubbed his jawline and rested his hands on his ivory gun grips. Defying his own nerves, he finally managed to speak as terror gripped his throat.

'Then who is it, Kid?' he asked.

Kid Cheyenne grinned as he returned to his coffee cup and gestured to Charlie Bart to refill it. He sat down as the sound of horses being halted came from just outside the Spinning Wheel.

'I told a couple of Casey's cowboys to round up as many of the Twisted Bar and Double C wranglers as they could find and come here to protect you, York,' he informed as he picked up the tin cup and blew at its steaming beverage.

York's smile was brief as he suddenly considered the likely outcome of his real cowboys tangling with Black and his gang of gunmen.

'But our cowhands ain't no match for Black's bunch, Kid,' he said as he sat back down and started to shake his head sadly. 'They'll all be killed in a shootout. Most of them couldn't hit the side of a barn

146

with a scattergun. They're just cowboys.'

The Kid lowered his cup from his lips and nodded.

'I know, York,' he muttered. 'But they know how to use their ropes don't they?'

Bart frowned. 'All cowboys know how to use their ropes but what chance would they have against gun-toting hombres like Black and his gang?'

Kid Cheyenne listened to the five veteran cowhands enter the otherwise deserted saloon and then smiled at both of the men seated across the card table from him.

'You'll find out,' he taunted.

TWENTY-FOUR

Kid Cheyenne glanced at the tobacco-stained clock on the saloon wall as it gave out a pathetic chime. He got to his feet, straightened his gun-belt and looked at the sleeping rancher and bartender, before turning to the five cowboys seated near the rear door of the Spinning Wheel. They were all wide awake as they sipped on their beers and watched the gunfighter stride toward them.

The Kid looked at the five cowboys. They were all weathered by countless years of handling steers in the merciless terrain and yet each of them looked ready to take on the unscrupulous Ben Black and his cohorts.

'It's nearly six by my reckoning,' he told the gathering as he pulled out his last cigar and bit off its tip. 'The sun will be rising soon and I figure that Black and his cronies will arrive not long after.'

'Are you sure they're coming back here, Kid?' asked one of the cowhands as beer suds dripped from his white moustache. 'Them galoots like to back-shoot

148

folks. Why would they risk a fight in the open?'

The Kid nodded in agreement and then scratched a match with his thumbnail. He sucked in smoke and then looked down on the seated cowboys.

'You're right about them being stinking cowards,' he agreed, before blowing a line of smoke at the floor. 'The thing is I kinda threatened Black. I told him that I want paying for coming all the way from Waco to this godforsaken place. Him and his gun-hands will be coming here on the pretext of paying me but I know their kind. They'll be coming here to bushwhack me.'

The cowboys did not say a word but they looked at one another gravely. They started to drink their beer faster as it began to dawn on them that they might not be around to enjoy too many more.

York awoke and looked around the saloon in a blind panic.

What he had thought was just a nightmare, was real. He picked up a cup of cold coffee and drained every drop of it before staring at Kid Cheyenne and the cowboys.

York got to his feet and shuffled to the last dregs of his and O'Hara's once formidable workforce. He nodded at the cowboys and then looked at the Kid.

'What the hell have you got planned, boy?' he asked.

'I've told these boys what I want them to do, York,' the Kid explained. 'The last thing I want is for them to get shot.'

The fiery old rancher moved closer to the tall gun-fighter and stared up into the Kid's eyes. He rested his knuckles on his hips and growled.

'If you don't want them getting shot then you shouldn't have told them to come here, Kid,' he snorted. 'Black ain't particular who he kills.'

Kid Cheyenne rested a hand on the shoulder of the rancher.

'If they just do what I've asked them to do, none of them will get killed,' he said. 'I didn't ask them to come here to be targets for Black and his cronies.'

Toke York's expression altered as he stared into the face of the notorious gunfighter. He knew when a man was being as honest as fate allowed, and as far as he could tell, the Kid was not lying.

The veteran rancher was about to speak when the Kid beat him to the punch.

'What time does the bank open around here?' he snapped.

'About eight thirty,' one of the cowboys piped up.

'The damn place closes around ten,' another chipped in.

The lean gunfighter looked back at the wall clock and shook his head. Time seemed to be moving a lot faster that it had before. He looked anxious as he turned his back on the rancher and the cowboys.

Kid Cheyenne pulled the cigar from his mouth and nodded as smoke billowed from his lips. He was thoughtful as he made his way toward the swing doors and rested an elbow on the top of its blistered wooden surface. He stared out into the quiet street.

'It'll be sun up soon by the look of that sky,' he informed the rest of the men inside the Spinning

Wheel. He looked at the cowboys. 'Get into position, boys.'

The five cowhands got to their feet and marched across the sawdust toward the Kid. One by one they left the saloon, pulled their long leathers free of the hitching pole and mounted.

One by one they touched their hat brims and rode in different directions. Toke York rushed to the side of the watching gunfighter and saw the cowboys disappear into the darkness. He looked at Kid Cheyenne.

'Where are they going, Kid?' he asked.

'You'll find out,' Kid Cheyenne drawled.

TWENTY-FIVE

Kid Cheyenne had never lured so many deadly gunmen to him before and wondered the wisdom of his decision. He usually faced his foes head on but this time it was different. The gunslinger moved well away from the Spinning Wheel as the first rays of the new day's sun started to spread its merciless light across Bloodstone and its surrounding areas.

The Kid walked around the settlement's seemingly empty streets in search of the perfect place in which to confront the deadly Black and company.

He exhaled as he reached the bank and paused beside its red brick façade. His eyes darted up and down the wide street but there seemed to be no place that seemed any safer than the next.

For the first time in his life, Kid Cheyenne was not confident of the outcome of this fight. He had never once doubted his gun skills but the man who called himself Ben Black and his hired guns had started to sap even the renowned gunslinger's confidence.

The Kid moved one building up from the bank to

the town's only hotel. He mounted the steps on the outside of the structure and walked to where the balcony gave him an uninterrupted view of everything between Bloodstone and the range. He knelt and looked out over the freshly painted railings at the lake. The rising sun danced off the water like a thousand fireflies to his weary eyes.

The Kid rubbed his face hard and tried to stay alert.

He stared through the gaps between the railings at the dust that was rising up into the heavens. His keen eyesight could make out that six riders and their mounts were kicking up the dust.

'They're coming,' he told himself grimly.

As he studied the horsemen, his mind flashed to the cowboys he had sent to various parts of the main thoroughfare. He wondered where they were. The Kid shielded his eyes against the blinding sunlight but grew no wiser.

Without their assistance, the Kid doubted if he could get the better of the half dozen horsemen who were riding towards the remote settlement.

He wiped sweat from his features and then removed his topcoat and revealed his holstered .45s. He returned back to his feet and walked the entire length of the hotel balcony, searching for the veteran cowhands.

'I sure hope they ain't high-tailed it,' he muttered as he finally reached the eastern corner of the hotel. He then glanced across at the small café and felt his innards tighten.

The Kid knew that the demure Olivia West had

arisen and was already downstairs in her small business. He gripped the top of the railings and knew that she was oblivious to what was about to happen in the normally quiet Bloodstone.

His heart quickened as he ran across the balcony and raced across the street toward the café. He leapt over the stream in the middle of the street and continued on to the eatery. As he reached the front door and grabbed its door handle he heard the unmistakable voice of Toke York bellowing out from beyond the Spinning Wheel. Whatever the rancher was yelling so feverishly, Kid Cheyenne could not fathom it.

Whatever York was trying to convey was lost in the morning air. It had reached its target though.

Kid Cheyenne hesitated for a second as he squinted through the almost blinding sunlight to where he had heard the voice of the rancher. Then he pushed the door inward and stepped into the café.

The handsome female looked from her cooking range at the man who had vowed to return. Her beaming smile soon changed as the Kid looked straight at her.

'Lock this door, Olivia,' he shouted frantically. 'Don't open it until I get back here and tell you it's safe. I ain't got time to explain, just lock up and keep your head low.'

Before she could respond, the Kid had closed the door and was running down the street in the direction of York's frantic voice. Olivia rushed to the café door and locked it back up just as the Kid had commanded. She had no idea what was going on but started to tremble as she feared the worst.

Kid Cheyenne had just reached the corner of the Spinning Wheel saloon when Toke York's voice stopped him in his tracks as he passed the alley.

'Kid,' York called out again. 'Get back here, boy.'

The gunfighter skidded to an abrupt halt and stared in bewilderment at the rancher. The Kid moved quickly to the side of York and stared down at him.

'What are you doing out here, Toke?' he growled. 'I told you and that barkeep to stay inside the saloon until the shooting stopped.'

'It ain't started yet, Kid,' York grunted. 'I just thought that you might like to know that Black and his boys have split up on the outskirts of town. Me and Charlie were upstairs when I spotted them Lazy B critters separate.'

The face of Kid Cheyenne went ashen.

'They done what?' he asked.

'Three riders headed around town while Black and two others kept on riding towards the end of the main street,' York informed breathlessly. 'I figured you ought to know otherwise they could get the drop on you.'

'You done good, Toke,' Kid Cheyenne patted the shoulder of the rancher in thanks and gritted his teeth as he considered his dwindling options. 'Now find cover before the gunplay erupts around here.'

'What you gonna do, boy?' York looked concerned.

The Kid did not reply. He was already running with guns drawn and heading for the bank to await the arrival of the infamous Ben Black.

FINALE

The alley beside the red brick structure was bathed in shadow as the rising sun quietly crept across the desert sand toward the awaiting Kid Cheyenne. The Kid cocked both his guns with his thumbs as he rested a shoulder against the solid bank wall and stared down the main street into the shimmering heat haze. It was hard to see anything as the air swirled before his narrowed eyes.

The Kid glanced around the long wide street in search of the five cowboys he had sent out from the saloon an hour or so earlier. Wherever they were, he could not see any of them. Beads of sweat trailed down from his hatband as the usually confident gunslinger began to doubt his crude plan.

Then, as he was about to move to a better hiding place, he saw the haze shimmer. Ben Black rode between two outriders like a man about to seize the throne of some ancient realm.

'Damn it all,' he growled as he watched the three horsemen suddenly break free of the hot haze. Each

156

rider had placed the stock of their rifles on their thighs in readiness as their metal barrels glinted in the sun. The Kid wondered where the other three of Black's small army had gone. He looked over his wide shoulders in fear of being bushwhacked. As his heart pounded like an Apache war drum inside his chest, he realized that it was pointless worrying about the men he could not see and he had to concentrate on the ones that he could.

He returned his icy stare at the approaching riders and then strode away from his hiding place. The Kid did not slow his pace as his long legs took him close to the flowing stream in the middle of the street.

The Kid placed a boot to either side of the fast-flowing water and then glared from under his hat brim at Black and his two riders. They were less than twenty feet from where the Kid was standing.

'That's far enough, Black,' Kid Cheyenne shouted along the otherwise silent street. 'You ain't going any further.'

Ben Black pulled back on his long leathers and stopped his mount. The pair of outriders also stopped and stared at the defiant Kid who was blocking their way.

Furiously, Black pulled a well-chewed cigar from his lips and threw it angrily at the sand. He steadied his mount as his trigger finger curled around the Winchester's trigger.

'What you gonna do if I decide to keep on coming, Kid?' he yelled at the gunslinger. 'You sure ain't gonna get paid no $20,000 if you kill me.'

Kid Cheyenne stared at Black and then recognized who the owner of the Lazy B actually was. He held his guns at arm's length and tilted his head back.

'You'd be right if it wasn't for the fact that you ain't actually Ben Black at all,' he shouted back at the horseman. 'I thought that I recognized you last night but it just occurred to me that your real name is Yancey Brooker.'

Black had not heard his true name for more than six years and it astounded him that the gunslinger would recall him. He gripped his rifle more tightly.

'I ain't ever heard of Yancey Brooker,' Black lied.

Kid Cheyenne took a step forward as his eyes darted between the three horsemen. 'Yancey Brooker is wanted for killing a rancher and his kinfolk back in Montana a while back. He disappeared after being branded as an outlaw wanted dead or alive. If my memory is correct I reckon you're worth at least $5,000.'

Ben Black screamed to his men. 'Kill him.'

The sun flashed off the rifle barrels as all three men swung their Winchesters down and trained them on the defiant gunslinger.

Before Black or his hirelings could start firing, the Kid had raised both his .45s and started squeezing his triggers.

His deadly aim managed to hit both men who flanked Black but before he had time to cock and shoot at the ominous rancher he had dropped to the ground between the horses.

As the outriders fell lifelessly from their mounts,

Black knelt between the skittish horses and blasted his rifle at the gunfighter. For the first time in his entire life, the Kid felt a bullet impact his shoulder.

He buckled to his knees but somehow kept firing his guns.

As rifle bullets whizzed repeatedly past the kneeling Kid Cheyenne, he gritted his teeth and aimed one of his six-shooters carefully.

The Kid pulled on the trigger and watched as Ben Black was knocked backwards by his perfectly aimed shot. As the rancher landed on his back, a fountain of crimson gore came from the fatal wound.

As the sound of the brief but bloody battle faded into the dust, Kid Cheyenne clambered back to his feet and started walking toward the three carcasses as the horses turned and cantered away.

He glanced at the smoking guns in his trembling hands.

Scarlet gore covered his left hand as the shoulder wound constantly pumped his lifeblood from the savage bullet hole. His shirt sleeve was stained as he holstered the gun and stared at his bloody hand. His eyes looked down upon the body of Ben Black at his feet and then he heard horses trotting behind his hunched shoulders.

Kid Cheyenne swung around on his heels and stared to where he could hear the distinctive sound of horses' hoofs approaching his pain-racked frame.

For a few heart-stopping moments his narrowed eyes could not see the horses but then they appeared. The five cowboys had roped the three remaining Lazy

B men with the expertise that only wranglers possessed. They dragged the three men behind their horses.

The Kid stared at their bloody remnants and sighed heavily.

He nodded to the cowboys and he heard Toke York's victorious cheers behind him as the veteran rancher ran toward the wounded gunslinger.

Reluctantly, Sheriff Green appeared from his office and moved towards the swaying Kid. He did not dare utter a word to Kid Cheyenne, who was still gripping one of his six-shooters in his hand. As the lawman paused above the body of Black, he glanced silently at the Kid.

'The critter you know as Ben Black is actually a hombre known as Yancey Brooker, sheriff,' the Kid sighed as his eyes watched the café door open and Olivia West run toward him. 'I claim the reward on that bastard. Wire the capitol and figure out how much you owe me exactly.'

Just as Harvey Green was about to speak, he was brushed aside by the running Olivia. Her arms wrapped around the Kid and she dragged his lips down to greet her own. As they parted he stared down into her sparkling eyes and smiled.

'Has this town got a doctor, ma'am?' he whispered.